Killer Hockey Mascot

Robbie Dorman

For RLM.

1

Gutsy stared, his enormous eyes never blinking.

Harvey stared back at the billboard, smoking a cigarette. Gutsy's face was front and center on it, big, red, with wobbly eyes and a huge mane of crimson fur.

Gutsy returned his stare at him, and Harvey broke his gaze away. He couldn't even look at the billboard. Harvey took another long drag from his cigarette and then snubbed it out. The rain fell beyond the confines of the patio of the bar, on the edge of downtown, across from the Brawlers' arena, where Harvey worked.

Where he *had* worked.

Not anymore. Not anymore.

Harvey returned to the interior of the bar and sat back down where he'd been all night.

"Another rum and coke," he said, sliding a twenty across the bar to the bartender, who nodded, pouring him a drink. Harvey couldn't afford it, not really. Without the paycheck from the Brawlers, he should save that money, and look for new work.

He couldn't afford to drink, no, not really.

But he couldn't afford not to, either.

The drinks were the only thing that kept Gutsy out of his thoughts.

The bartender slid the booze over to him, made change, and vanished again, down to the other end of the bar, to talk to the pretty girl who sat alone. Harvey didn't blame him. Harvey had tried to talk to him, but no matter where the conversation started, it always came back to the damn mascot. To the Brawlers. To Gutsy.

Jen had left because of it. No matter what they were doing, when he wasn't working, he'd only talk about work. And not even about work. He'd talk about Gutsy.

She didn't understand, she couldn't understand.

She hadn't worn the costume. She hadn't slid Gutsy's head over hers. She hadn't seen—

—the Red—

Harvey swallowed down the rum and coke quickly. He didn't want his buzz to disappear, he wanted it louder, to drown out those thoughts that returned time and time again to that stupid mascot, seven feet tall, who he had embodied for a few months. He left the bar. He needed to go for a walk, get away from that billboard, he could feel Gutsy's eyes on him, he knew that damn thing was watching him—

Harvey walked out into the drizzling rain. It was a miserable night, but he could deal with the rain. He could deal with anything.

He walked away from the arena, toward the rest of downtown. He hadn't thought to come back here, not really, but he had, he had told himself to drink, but was it that? There were plenty of bars near his apartment. He didn't need to come here to drink. Had it been Gutsy that pulled him here?

No, that was impossible. Stupid. It was just a mascot.

Just a mascot.

Jen hadn't understood. Harvey hadn't wanted her to leave. He had needed her, more than ever, but he understood why she left. It was the same reason he quit. He couldn't take it anymore. He should call her. Tomorrow, he would call. See how she felt. See if she would give him another chance.

He walked, the rain pelting him. He was thinking about going to another bar, but for now he was happy to walk, the warm glow of the alcohol working through him.

But it wasn't enough to banish Gutsy from his thoughts.

He hadn't told Shannon he was quitting. He couldn't face her. Harvey knew why he didn't want to tell her, why he had ghosted her, why he hadn't answered her texts. She was the only other person who could understand what it was like. She knew what it felt like to *be* Gutsy. To see through that red fur.

He felt guilty for leaving her to do the job alone. They were a team, that's what she had said, and he had agreed, they were a team, they couldn't work without each other, but he had left, he'd had to leave, for his own sanity.

It was too much. What it felt like with the suit on. What the world looked like. The feelings followed him, even without the costume on. Even when he wasn't Gutsy, he still carried them.

And that's not even touching on his dreams.

No, not dreams.

Nightmares.

Harvey walked. He ducked under an awning, and lit up another cigarette, the nicotine high keeping him alert, the balancing act against the booze.

He wandered without direction, the rain pelting him. The rain picked up, but Harvey stayed out in it, and turned down a street, and then turned again at the next corner. He suddenly found himself at the edge of downtown, facing the arena again. He couldn't escape it. The billboard loomed over him.

Gutsy stared.

Harvey turned from it and walked quickly, puffing on his cigarette. He had to get away from that damn *thing*, he didn't even know why he came downtown, he should have stayed in his apartment, and searched for jobs—

He turned again, and he was walking through an alley. He could get back to his car this way, he thought, but then he heard a shuffling noise behind him, and he stopped, and turned.

Nothing. The alley was empty, aside from him, a dumpster, and a few boxes.

Must have been the rain.

But Harvey's mind went to the murders. It was only a few people, and in a big city, it was easy to rationalize. There was no danger. He kept his head on a swivel. He minded his own business. No one would bother him.

Harvey's eyes stayed glued to the dumpster. Did it just move?

No. Of course not.

He felt the sudden urge to run. To sprint out the other end of the alley, to find his car, to jump inside and drive away. To go home, dry off, and start his search for a new job tomorrow. He'd call Jen, set his life straight, and leave Gutsy behind.

Harvey didn't run, though. His legs urged him to, his knees tightened, ready to move, but he resisted. Something told him that if he ran, he would be cut down in the alley, never seeing what killed him. It didn't make sense, but still, he listened.

He didn't run. Instead, he crept toward the dumpster, in the dim alley, the heavy rain pouring down. There was nothing there, he was sure. But he wouldn't turn his back on it, not until he knew.

He inched forward, and now he could smell the trash inside the container, the lid pulled off, the rain soaking the garbage. He glanced in, and there was nothing but trash. Harvey had heard the noise from the other side of the dumpster.

There was nothing there, he knew it.

He would find nothing, he would leave this alley, and go back to his life.

The cigarette burned down to the filter in his hand, and he dropped it with a flare of pain between his fingers, but he didn't look, he couldn't look away, and he finally saw the other side of the dumpster, and there was nothing there.

There was nothing there, and then he heard the noise again, and he turned, and Gutsy stood there, looming over him.

"No—" he started, and then Gutsy's spade hand reached inside him, and his guts spilled out into the alley, and the rain poured down on him. It was impossible, they were just nightmares, Gutsy was just a costume, just a costume.

Gutsy said nothing, his eyes staring at him. Gutsy stared at Harvey as he opened his mouth wide, wider than possible, and swallowed everything that Harvey was.

2

"Do you have any experience working as a mascot?"

Tom smiled as confidently as his face would allow. "Yes, I was friends with Mickey at Disney World, when I lived in Orlando."

"Friends with Mickey?"

"That's the code you're taught to use. You don't play Mickey. You're friends with him," said Tom. The interviewer chuckled. She sat across from him in a small conference room, his resume in front of her.

"Is that right?" she asked. "I didn't realize."

"Absolutely true," said Tom. And it was. And he hadn't technically lied on his resume, when he said he had worked for Disney for two years, and he *had* been friends with Mickey. Sure, the majority of that time had been spent working as a cashier, after he graduated into the worse job market since the 70s, and there were no jobs, anywhere, except selling ice cream to tourists. He'd only played Mickey Mouse for a week, and then quit when he got a better job where he didn't sweat in the Florida sun for meager pay.

"I see you have an English degree," said Barbara—he thought she'd said her name was Barbara. She had blonde hair, and wore a blouse and a long skirt, and Tom would say whatever she wanted to hear as long as she hired him. He needed this damn job, even if it was to play Gutsy. He had no real desire to play the meme mascot, but he needed the paycheck. Tom owed three thousand dollars in back due rent.

"And you've worked in theater?"

"Oh, yes," he said, smiling again, making eye contact. The Wall Street Journal top ten tips on interviews flashed through his mind. He'd read it through before he left this morning. "Big fan of the theater. I see a lot of similarities in working as Gutsy. It's a live crowd, you're in costume, you have to play your part." He didn't mention that it'd been community theater, getting paid in donuts that the director would bring in the morning. Or that he'd only played an extra. She didn't need to know that.

"That's a good point," said Barbara. She scribbled a note. Was that good? He hoped so. "You have a degree in creative writing?"

"Yes."

"How do you think that will help you with this position?" she asked, a rote question about how his impractical degree would support him playing a hockey muppet.

"My degree gives me a strong skill set for playing Gutsy.

It's creative, which is obviously important when you're trying to entertain. It also gave me a lot of experience receiving feedback and improving my work, which is important in any field, not just this position." Barbara's eyes were down, and looked bored—*wow her, Tom, put it all together*—"Coupled with my background in theater, and my experience performing in a mascot costume, it gives me all the skills necessary to play the part successfully."

Barbara took more notes and smiled as she looked at him. He hoped it was good.

"And you have reliable transportation to the arena?" she asked.

"Yes," he said, stretching the word reliable to its breaking point. His Civic *reliably* needed brake fluid replaced every other day or it wouldn't stop, but it drove. If he got the job, he'd get the brake line fixed, after he caught up on his rent, and his credit card bill, and his—

"That's all my questions," she said. "Are you ready to try on the suit?"

"What? We're doing that today?" he asked. "I thought—"

"Well, we need to know how it fits, if you're comfortable inside of it, and obviously, how well you perform with it on. Like you said, performance is the most important thing."

"Yes, of course," he said. He had let the word interview trick him, because it wasn't really an interview. It was an audition. He hadn't planned any performance.

Fuck.

"Follow me," said Barbara, and they left the small room and went down hallway after hallway, in the depths of the arena. It was early in the morning, so there were only a few other people they passed, all wearing gray uniforms, all doing their best to avoid looking at him.

They came to an unmarked door, and Barbara used the pass card around her neck, flashing next to an electronic lock, and it *hzzed* open. She went in and he followed and there, sitting unceremoniously in the corner was Gutsy. Or at least the different parts of Gutsy. His fuzzy crimson legs, his bulbous furry torso. His long neck that led to his cartoonish head, with a big mane of long red hair that hung from it, matched by a fiery beard. And finally, his eyes.

Tom stared into them, into the inanimate eyes. They were enormous, and bobbly. When someone was in the costume, they moved around constantly, while seeming to stay still, a feat that worked to make Gutsy the viral star he had become. His eyebrows completed the story, huge hairy caterpillars that tufted up, and made Gutsy look furiously angry almost all the time.

Gutsy had seized the world by storm. Tom didn't care one lick about hockey, and knew only to avoid the area around the Brawler's arena during game nights, because traffic was always bad. But Tom knew about Gutsy, just because of viral memes that got passed around online. He had thought they were funny, but then had quickly forgotten about them, until a new one popped up. Tom couldn't name a single professional hockey player except for Wayne Gretzky, but he knew Gutsy.

When he saw the ad on LinkedIn to perform as Gutsy, he had put it in his maybe pile for the day. He'd been applying for days on end, for anything that didn't involve having to talk directly to customers. His last five jobs had all been retail or service industry, and he'd been fired from all five. He inevitably would be a smart-ass to a customer, and do it too many times, and his manager would pull the lever that dropped Tom through the trapdoor into unemployment. It wasn't worth what little money they paid for hours he couldn't predict.

He had put the Gutsy job into the maybe pile because he was unqualified for it, but it paid decent money, and it kept him away from customers. He would have to interact with the fans, though. But—and it was a big but—no one would ever see his face. And Gutsy was allowed to be a jerk. It seemed to be encouraged, from all the videos he watched. He tweaked his resume, stretching the truth as far as he could, and sent it in, and forgot about it. Until he got a call from Barbara, asking if he was available to interview—well, audition.

Tom's eyes stayed locked with Gutsy's as they approached the costume.

"Wow," he said. It was huge. It must be seven feet tall. He didn't realize it when watching videos.

"Cool being this close, right?" asked Barbara. She had mistaken his intent, but he didn't correct her.

"Oh, yeah, absolutely," he said. "How do I—"

"I'll help you put it on," she said. "Normally, you'd wear athletic clothes beneath, but today, since it'll only be a few minutes, you're fine with what you have." He looked down at his slacks and button-down shirt.

"Shoes on or off?" he asked.

"Off," she said, and handed him the legs first. He slipped off his shoes and stepped into the legs, roughly the same size as his own. He remembered the rigmarole of putting on the Mickey costume, and how unpleasant it was to wear. At least he would be in a chilly hockey arena with it on.

Barbara held the bulbous torso in her arms.

"Arms up," she said, and Tom put his arms up as she slid the torso onto him. "It's a little awkward, but find the armholes, and slide your arms through into the sleeves." Tom found himself in darkness, the torso surrounding him, and he reached in the dark and found the holes, forcing his arms through, before his head popped out the neck hole, Gutsy's crimson mane fluffing around him, up to his nose, slightly in his vision. His right arm went through the sleeve easily, into the glove at the end, but his left arm got stuck, and he had to awkwardly pull on it with the cartoonish mitt that was now his right hand. He eventually got it on.

"Alright," said Barbara, smiling. She had grabbed the neck and head, easily a foot long, the most exaggerated thing in the costume, the massive eyes staring directly at Tom. "Are you ready?"

"Where are the eyes?" asked Tom.

"There's two thin spots in the neck that you'll look out of," said Barbara. "You might have to twist it around a little, until you can see."

"Understood. Let's do it," said Tom. Barbara placed the long, big neck over his head, and there was a foam insert inside that fit over his head. He wiggled it around, and something caught inside on his left ear, and he bent and moved and then it slid into place, and he cautiously opened his eyes.

The world was red.

He saw out through the red fabric that covered Gutsy's extended neck, giving him the exaggerated height that had struck Tom. The inner sleeve for the neck had a couple large cutouts for his eyes, and after a little shifting, he could see well through the holes. Everything had a red tint to it, like seeing in infrared.

He felt Gutsy's head balanced above him, and he'd have to be careful with his center of gravity, or otherwise, he'd tip over. He took a cautious step and felt himself list to one side, and he did his best to correct—he felt like a newborn deer, he wasn't used to being seven feet tall, Jesus Christ, he was going to fail this audition, he couldn't even move in this thing, not to mention doing bits in it—

But then something clicked in his head, a connection he hadn't felt before, something *red* sliding inside, and he corrected his movement.

Suddenly, the ruby tinted vision became clear in his mind's eye. After just a few moments, he felt the mascot body around him, and understood where and how it worked. He corrected his listing.

He felt—he felt at home. The big bulbous body was an extension of himself.

"How does it feel?" asked Barbara.

"It feels—good," said Tom. And it did. He had expected to feel awkward inside, but the suit fit like a glove, even with his business casual clothes on underneath. And after that first wave of awkwardness wore off, it felt like an extension of him. He could only see a small part of the world through his red-tinted glasses, but he sensed more, somehow. He couldn't explain it.

"Great!" said Barbara, smiling. "Follow me, as best you can, and we'll go to the audition area, where you can show me your stuff."

"Sounds good," said Tom, imbuing his voice with as much confidence as he could muster. But inside, he panicked. What the hell could he do in this costume? He'd seen mascots prance around, and do bits with kids, but he couldn't recycle normal stuff. That wouldn't get him hired—would it?

Then the panic subsided, the anxiety replaced with a calm peace. With confidence. The same confidence that he'd felt about his movement, he felt about his routine. He didn't know what he would do, but it didn't matter. It would work.

He followed Barbara inside Gutsy, ambling along, ducking just below low doorways.

Barbara kept looking back, checking on him.

"You're keeping up," she said. "You're a natural in that. The last few people kept falling over."

"It was a little awkward at first, but I've got a hang of it now," said Tom, projecting his voice out of the suit.

"You're doing great," she said, and then pushed through a door, and they were out in a more open area, and then Tom realized it was the concourse of the arena, where people would walk through to get to their seats, and go to the bathroom, and buy concessions. It was empty except for them.

Barbara walked over to a nearby wall.

"Here are some props we use for Gutsy's performances," she said. "You obviously don't have to have a whole routine, but I'd like to see what you're capable of." She smiled and gestured to the props, leaning up against the wall.

Tom looked at them, his mind working at connecting them. There was a hockey stick, a handful of pucks on the ground, a beach ball, a pool noodle, a sled, and a box, that Tom assumed had more random stuff inside of it. Should he root around in it? Did she expect him to take some time with this?

Then an idea formed in his mind, like lightning, and he remembered all the clips he'd seen of Gutsy, and thought to his amble, and remembered his eyes, and knew what to do. His mind shifted.

He *was* Gutsy.

He sauntered over to all the props and started his routine. He could see it all in his mind's eye.

Gutsy grabbed the hockey stick and carefully laid it up against the wall. He grabbed the pool noodle, and did the same, right next to it, loosely leaning.

Gutsy grabbed the sled, and he stared at it, and then threw it as far as he could without looking. He heard it clatter behind him. He picked up the beach ball, and squeezed it once, before hurling it as well. It bounced away, down the enormous hall.

He slowly picked up each puck, examining each one, before flinging them aside, until only one remained, which he carefully placed next to the hockey stick and the pool noodle.

He looked over at the big cardboard box, held his gaze for a second, and then sauntered over to it. He took a glance inside, and then grabbed it with both hands and upended it, and kicked it away. Now there was only the hockey stick, the pool noodle, and the lone puck.

He finally looked back over at Barbara. She looked amused, which was perfect. He gestured for her to come over with a single beckoning finger, and after a moment, she obliged. He gestured again to the hockey stick.

"For me?" she asked. He nodded, feeling Gutsy's gigantic head above him nod. She grabbed the hockey stick, and then he took the pool noodle. He grabbed the puck, and then moved it to the middle of the area, with plenty of room. He gestured to the puck, and then got into the stance for the faceoff, with his pool noodle held ready to swat at the puck. Barbara eyed him and he eyed her right back, with Gutsy's mean mug. He nodded as if he was counting—

1...

2...

3!

And then he ignored the puck and swatted at her with the pool noodle, circling her with the soft foam bopping off of her. Barbara laughed as he hopped around her, his eyes wobbling back and forth, the noodle bouncing off of her arms and shoulders.

"You win, you win," she said, and then walked over and put the hockey stick against the wall. Gutsy raised the noodle in victory before doing celebratory pelvic thrusts.

She walked back over to him.

"Let's get that head off of you," she said, and grabbed Gutsy by the top of his head.

For a second—

For a second, it felt like Tom's head was being ripped off, and he wanted to yell, but then the foam padding shifted, and it slid off him, and he closed his eyes from instinct, and when he opened them, the world was normal again, and he was just Tom again.

"How was it?" asked Barbara.

"It felt—right," said Tom. "It felt good." His mind reached for the appropriate words. It felt like he just woke up, and his brain was catching up.

"Did you plan that?" she asked.

"No," said Tom. "It just came to me. I put the suit on, and

I kind of—became Gutsy, I guess."

"It was great," said Barbara. "Quite frankly, it blew away what the other auditions have done."

"I—" started Tom. "That's great to hear. When can I expect to hear back?"

"Well, there's a home game tomorrow," said Barbara.

Tom looked at her, confused. "Okay? So, after that?"

"Oh, no," said Barbara. "You've got the job. Can you work the game tomorrow?"

3

"C'mon kid, I'll give you the dime tour." Tom followed Skates McTavish as he limped down the hallway. Barbara had introduced them, and then vanished, and now Skates slowly walked ahead of him, into the bowels of the arena.

Skates limped ahead, wearing loose khakis and a black Brawlers polo. Tom would bet that Skates used to be taller than him, but now he walked stooped. Skates had a small tousled bit of white hair up top, and the smallest amount of stubble on his face. Tom guessed Skates was in his mid-60s, but he wasn't going to ask.

Skates pointed to a door to the left, simply marked OF-FICE and opened it. "This here, this is my office. Taj Mahal, I tell ya." Skates spoke with a midwestern accent that Tom couldn't precisely identify.

"It's—"

Skates slammed the door shut.

"It's a room with a chair in it, which is what I mostly need from an office. Let's keep movin'," he limped ahead, not slowing down or speeding up, his pace exactly the same. "I have another secret spot, where I can relax. Don't tell no one."

"I wouldn't—"

"I know the place seems big, but after a while, you'll know all its secrets," said Skates. "Just remember the places I show ya today, and everything else will fill in eventually." He kept moving, pointing out bathrooms, and the different concourses, and where the public wasn't allowed to go.

"Mr. McTavish—"

"Whoa, whoa, kid," he said. "Call me Skates. Unless ya're my banker, call me Skates."

"Skates," said Tom. "You're—you're my boss, right? Barbara wasn't quite clear—"

"Eh, don't worry about her," said Skates. "She only worries about the big picture. Doesn't want to get her fingers dirty down here on the floor. Don't blame her, y'know. But yeah, technically, you report to me."

"Technically?"

"I'm an equipment manager, kid," said Skates, still moving. "I mostly worry if the players got the right skates, the right sticks, and clean sweaters. If their helmet fits the ways they like. I'm not a director. If you need something, come to me. Otherwise, you and Shannon can work out what you need to do. You don't need me telling you how to entertain the fans, y'know. Do your thing, and find me if your paycheck don't get direct deposited on time. Got it?"

"Got it," said Tom. "Where's the next stop?"

"Eh, there's not a whole lot more to show. I'll let Shannon fill you in on all the nitty gritty about that big red idiot. But I gotta introduce you to Cloudy before I hand you off to Shannon."

"Cloudy?" asked Tom.

"You not a Brawlers fan?" asked Skates as they moved down a hallway.

"No," said Tom. "I mean, nothing against them. I don't follow hockey."

"Guess you don't need to know about odd-man rushes to play that big moron," said Skates. "Well, you're a member of the team now, so you have to talk to Cloudy."

"Who—who's Cloudy?" asked Tom.

"I think he's getting his knee looked at," said Skates. He moved to a door that said MEDICAL on it and tapped twice before going in. "Everyone decent in here?"

"We're trying our best," said a deep voice. "Can't say the same for you, Skates. Last time you were decent, I was a baby."

Skates laughed like hell as they walked into the room. A trainer was examining a player sitting on the table. The man was huge, even sitting down, especially in his legs. He was a handsome dude, with a short beard and a fashionable haircut, brown hair trimmed on the sides, with a little left on top, wet and tousled to the side. He stuck out a hand for Skates and Skates shook it.

"You know that's a lie," said Skates. "You weren't even born when I was decent. Cloudy, this is our newest recruit. Tom Reynolds, this is Tanner Cloud, but everyone calls him Cloudy."

Cloud extended his hand, and Tom shook it, Cloud's hand enveloping his. Tom did his best to match the firmness of his strength, but he couldn't.

"Welcome to the team," said Cloudy, wincing as the trainer put pressure on his knee. "Playing the red guy, huh?"

"Yeah," said Tom. "Should be fun."

"You and Woody get the fans amped up," said Cloudy. "Amped up fans give us an advantage."

"Woody?" asked Tom.

"Shannon," said Skates. "Shannon's last name is Wood."

"You not a hockey guy?" asked Cloudy.

"No, not really," said Tom. "Nothing against it, just never a fan."

"Well, you'll learn quick, being here. We'll get you a nickname, if you stick around long enough. You have any trouble you can't handle, you find me, and we'll get it sorted out. We're a family."

"Uh, thanks," said Tom.

"I gotta get you to Shannon," said Skates.

"Nice meeting you," said Tom, and then they were back in the hallway, Skates still trailing a leg but not slowing down.

"Woody?" asked Tom.

"Hockey nicknames are the dumbest shit in the world," said Skates. "I love 'em. My given name isn't Skates, if you're wondering."

"Can I ask why—"

"Because I used to be the fastest player on the ice," said Skates, looking back at Tom and smirking, and then he led Tom to another door, into a small break room, where a woman sat in a plastic chair, staring at her phone.

"Hey, Skates," she said. "Is this the new guy?"

"This is him," said Skates. "Shannon, Tom. Tom, Shannon. Shannon is the other person who plays Gutsy. I'll leave you with her. I gotta get back to work. There's a game tonight." Tom turned and then Skates was gone, leaving him alone with Shannon.

Shannon still looked at her phone. She looked in her mid-30s, with shoulder length brown hair. She wore khakis and a Brawlers polo, which he guessed was game day uniform. Shannon looked like she'd rather be anywhere else.

"You gonna sit down?" asked Shannon, still not looking at him.

"I thought we needed to get ready for the game," said Tom.

"It's not even noon, man," said Shannon. "Game doesn't start until eight, and I'll be in costume at six. We need to rehearse a spot, but it'll take maybe half an hour. You were smart enough to fool Barbara into hiring you, so you're smart enough to learn the spot in thirty minutes. Take a seat and I'll tell you what you need to know."

Tom shrugged and sat across from Shannon at the break table.

"What do I need to know?"

Shannon finally stopped looking at her phone.

"Skates is a great boss, so don't abuse privileges, or you'll ruin it for both of us. They want us here early on game days, but most times you just have to sit here on your phone, or with a book. You still get paid. Normally, we alternate wearing the suit. When you're not in the suit, you'll be the handler, in case somebody tries to start a fight, or the suit needs to get through a tight space. Also, when either of us isn't in the costume, we'll serve as an extra in bits during the game. Don't break character when you're Gutsy, and never allow anyone to see you without the head on. It fits pretty damn tight, so it's not too much of a concern. Have you worn a mascot costume before?"

"I was Mickey in Disney World," said Tom. "Briefly."

"Good enough," said Shannon. "Gutsy is the most comfortable costume I've worn, but it still gets hot after a few hours, even in the arena. There're little fans inside the suit, but they don't work very well, so I normally don't turn them on because they smell. We get the same food the players get, so you don't have to bring meals on game day unless you want to. Don't socialize with the players unless they start it. The players largely don't care, and Cloudy is everyone's best friend, but Barbara and all of them don't like us mingling in our off-hours, for whatever reason. I think that's everything important. Have any questions?"

"I don't think so," said Tom. "Well—"

"What is it?" asked Shannon.

"You seem annoyed that I'm here," said Tom. "Did I do something wrong?"

Shannon opened her mouth to speak, and then closed it, opened it again. "Sorry. I'm tired. I didn't sleep well last night. You're the fourth new guy we've had in a month, so—" She paused. "So, I've had to do this a lot lately. Constantly having new co-workers is very tiring, especially when I'm teaching them all the same thing."

"I'm the fourth new guy?" asked Tom. "What happened to them?"

"They've all quit," said Shannon. "Ghosted."

"Did they say why?"

"No," said Shannon. "They just didn't show up. They didn't answer the phone, or texts. It gets very—frustrating. So I'm sorry if I seem rude. But there's a part of me that is just expecting you to quit."

"Is there anything I should know about the job?" asked Tom. "Anything that could cause people to quit, let's say?"

Shannon paused, for just a moment. "No. I've worked here since the team introduced Gutsy. It's not the best job in the world, but it pays the bills."

"Well, I have no intention of quitting," said Tom.

"That's good to hear, at least," said Shannon. "We should get our bit for later ready. Follow me."

Shannon got up and walked out of the break room. Tom followed.

"We don't need the suit for this," said Shannon. "But I'll wear it tonight, so you get a sense of what it's like to be out and about in it, and general behavior. If you're ready, you can wear it for Thursday's game."

Shannon led him to an upper concourse, to a set of seats near the edge of the seating, where it dropped off to the next level.

"We'll do the bit we always do with the new guys," said Shannon. "You'll sit here." She gestured to a seat. "Our crowd person, Amy, during the first intermission, will announce that we're celebrating a birthday."

"And I'll be the one celebrating," said Tom.

"You got it," said Shannon. "I'll come up, as Gutsy, carrying a big sheet cake. I'll hand it over to you. You need to act really excited. Amy will ask you your name and how old you are. You answer, and then she'll start everyone singing Happy Birthday."

"And at the end of the song, I get a face full of cake, right?" asked Tom.

"Right," said Shannon. "Do you want to practice?"

"Do we really need to?" asked Tom. "I've seen the bit done. I can do it."

"You sure?" asked Shannon.

"Yeah, I think so," said Tom.

*

"We're celebrating a birthday today," boomed across the arena. Tom stood next to Amy, at the same exact spot. He tried to look oblivious to everything, while simultaneously excited.

The crowd cheered at the announcement.

"What's your name, and how old are you turning?" asked Amy.

"Uh, I'm Adam, and I'm turning 30 years old," he said, adding a bit of excitement and shyness.

"Dirty thirty," said Amy. "Well, for your thirtieth birthday, the Brawlers and a very special someone prepared something just for you."

Then Gutsy appeared, walking up from a stairway, a massive cake in his arms.

"Look who it is!" yelled Amy, and the crowd cheered, as Gutsy's angry, rage-filled eyes led the way. He walked over to Tom, and slowed down, the crowd waiting to see what he would do. Tom played the part. He smiled and openly accepted the cake, playing up to the fans that he was a schmuck, and building up their anticipation that he'd get the cake right away.

But Gutsy handed it off into Tom's waiting arms. The cake was big, two feet across, and he held it out in two arms like a cord of firewood.

Amy smiled. "Gutsy made this cake just for you. Now everyone here, let's sing Happy Birthday for Adam!" Amy started singing, and the crowd joined in. Tom stood there, holding the cake, smiling like a dope, but inside, he had to admit it was neat having fifteen thousand people sing "Happy Birthday" to him.

Gutsy stood nearby, waving his arms like he was conducting the crowd. He grew more and more animated as they neared the final lyrics.

Happy Birthday to Yooooooou!

They sang out, and Shannon hit her cue perfectly, and flipped the cake directly into Tom's face, smashing the cake all over him, and holding it there.

The crowd cheered and laughed, all at once, and Tom enjoyed it, despite the fact that his face, mouth, and nose were filled with cake. He waited a few moments, waited for Shannon to stop rubbing it in his face, so he could breathe again, but the moments passed, and Gutsy still held the cake on his face, and he tried to struggle away, but Gutsy held the cake firm, and he tried to breathe, but there was only cake, in his throat, in his sinuses, and he felt himself flounder, struggling to breathe, *oh fuck, he was going to choke to death in front of fifteen thousand people*, and then finally, the cake was down, and he coughed, once, twice, and he could breathe again.

Jesus, Shannon, you nearly killed me.

He did his best to get back into character, although his lungs still ached. Amy gestured to him, and they retreated quickly, and with the cameras off him, everyone forgot. They disappeared through a door into the innards of the arena. Shannon would spend a little more time entertaining the crowd, but his night was done. He cleaned himself off, and took a shower, and by the time he had washed up, the game was over. The Brawlers had won a close game—three to two.

Shannon sat at their break table, Gutsy's head in front of her. She looked beat.

"You okay?" he asked. His job was over for the day, but he wanted to wait around until Shannon was done with hers. It felt only right.

"I'm alright," she said. But she didn't look alright. She looked exhausted. Sure, he knew wearing the suit for a couple hours was hard, but Shannon looked on the verge of collapse. "Becoming Gutsy always takes a lot out of me."

"You know, you scared me with the cake bit," said Tom.

"What do you mean?"

"I mean, I felt like I was about to choke to death on the cake."

"You should have given me the high sign," said Shannon.

"I tried to!" said Tom. "It wasn't easy with sinuses full of icing. I tried to push the cake away, but you weren't having it."

"I'm—I'm sorry," she said. "I didn't mean to."

"It's not a big deal," said Tom. "Just a little scary." He stood up. "If it's okay, I'm going to head home."

"You're good to go," said Shannon. "I can close up without you."

"See you tomorrow," said Tom, and went to leave.

"I *am* sorry," said Shannon as he left.

"No worries," said Tom, turning back toward her. "It was our first time working together."

"That's true," said Shannon. "Sometimes, when I'm in the suit, I *become* Gutsy, if you know what I mean." She took a breath. "And Gutsy—Gutsy doesn't always want to let up."

4

"You ready to go?" asked Shannon.

Tom sat at the break table. He wore the Gutsy suit. Well, he wore the Gutsy suit, except for the head. The head sat in front of him, staring at him. He stared back, into Gutsy's rage filled eyes, the eyebrows tufting up into the air.

"Yeah, just psyching myself up," he said.

"You'll do fine out there," said Shannon. "Just follow the route in your head, and before you know it, we'll be sitting here, about to go home." Shannon wore a black suit, with black Ray-Bans. Gutsy's handler was always dressed in the suit, to appear more authoritative. Also made Gutsy look like a wild animal that needed suits to control. Worked on multiple levels.

"I hope so," said Tom. "Doesn't help my nerves."

"If you need a break, just walk away, throwing your arms up in the air. Gutsy is flighty and impulsive, so it gives you the freedom to take a breath. If you desperately need to get out of the suit, for any reason, grab my face with your hands, and whisper that you need out. I'll make a big fuss and then lead you away. We can duck out into the hallways somewhere, and give you a moment without the head on, at least."

"I'll keep that in mind," said Tom. "But I don't want to have that as a crutch. I just want to do the job."

"You're still learning," said Shannon. "Pushing yourself too hard won't help anybody."

"Fair enough," said Tom. "Help me with the head?"

Shannon helped him slide it on, and once again, the world went red. Different from before, because he wore the proper athletic gear on underneath the suit, but not that different. The head slid into place, and Tom stood up. He took a few cautious steps and then the same feeling fell over him, just like during his audition. He moved and Gutsy moved with him, and after those first few steps, he *was* Gutsy, moving his arms and legs and head, feeling in and above him at the same time. Feeling his gigantic eyes above him, staring out into the world.

Shannon led the way, in her suit, and pushed open the door and then they were in the concourse, and there were fans everywhere, and Tom truly became Gutsy for the first time. People immediately cheered and whooped as Gutsy walked past them. Shannon was leading him to an area that had been cordoned off for photo ops. He would be swarmed if he just walked around the concourse as thousands of people streamed in to see the game that night.

Even with Shannon leading the way, and other staff helping control the crowd, it was still thick with people. Tom did his best to stay in character, reacting as everyone took impromptu videos or selfies with him.

Tom had expected himself to be anxious around this many people, but he wasn't. He was—the opposite, actually. He felt assured. He felt confident.

He felt powerful.

He swaggered through the crowd, Gutsy did, and soon they were in the photo op area, with a Brawlers themed backdrop, and statues of Brawlers greats nearby. Tom had no idea who they were, but he assumed they were Brawlers greats.

He was in a roped-off area now, and a little more free to entertain. He posed, and pelvic thrusted, which earned a pop from the crowd. The line was already sizable. Everyone wanted a picture with Gutsy. A small nod to Shannon and she started letting people through, one person, two people, families, all coming in to meet Gutsy.

It was a blur, a multitude of faces, all wanting a moment with Gutsy. Tom did his best to deliver. He used everything in the mascot bag of tricks, plus a few extra, ones that only Gutsy could get away with, like pulling off people's hats and throwing them away.

Group after group came through the area, and Tom entertained them, even as they all looked red. A good portion of them were already drunk, probably from tailgating out in the parking lot. It was cold as hell outside, but that didn't stop a select group of fans from pre-gaming. But still, they were easy to handle. They might be a little handsy, but Shannon and the rest of the event staff were there to pull away anyone that wanted to get involved. Tom kept his antics to a minimum with the drunk folks, and they mostly would wander away to soak up their booze with some hot dogs.

Tom had taken the job for the paycheck, but he still found it rewarding to entertain the children who stopped by, even if some of them were completely terrified of him. He didn't blame them. Gutsy towered over them, seven feet tall. Gutsy was otherworldly, with big red tufts of crimson hair, and some kids thought he was just another Sesame Street character. Others thought he was the Devil.

Either way, parents would usher their little ones to get a picture with Gutsy, and some would hug him. He'd hug them back.

Others would bawl their eyes out, screaming in terror. Parents pushed them toward him still, and Tom couldn't tell them that their child was clearly scared of him as the big red beast, and maybe you should wait until next year for a picture.

But he said nothing, and the parade of people continued.

"Look at this fucking thing," said the voice loudly, and Tom looked at the man sauntering up to him, a small woman in tow. Boyfriend/girlfriend? Husband/wife? Tom didn't know, but the man's voice carried across the entire concourse. Tom didn't expect any sports arena to be a paradigm of clean language, but little kids stood not ten feet away. The man was large, over six feet tall, with a big gut, a hockey jersey stretched over it. He carried a shopping bag, fresh from the team store. He wore a flat brimmed Brawlers hat, tucked low on his big head.

"You sure you want a picture with the ugly fucking muppet?" yelled the man again.

"Yes, yes," said the woman, a tiny blonde wearing a jersey as well. Tom didn't know if the man was drunk or not. He wasn't slurring his words or stumbling. Some people were rude and loud regardless if they were drinking or not.

"Well, let's hurry it up," said the man.

"Yes, Sam," said the woman.

Tom eyed him through the red cloth and quickly got into position to take a picture for the photographer.

"What, we can't use our own camera?" Sam yelled.

"I'm sorry, sir," said Shannon, stepping in. "You'll be able to find the shots on our Facebook page."

"Jesus fucking Christ," he said. "All of this for your damn social media. Hurry the fuck up, Marcia. I got a game to watch."

"Not everything is about you, Sam," said Marcia, quietly.

Tom took a deep breath inside of Gutsy. He remembered his brief time as Mickey. No one saw his face, so they treated him like he wasn't there. Treated him like he didn't hear whatever they said. Even in a week as Mickey, he'd heard people whisper horrible things, just because Mickey wasn't real, and Mickey wouldn't be able to tell anyone.

"What the fuck did you say?" asked Sam, but this time his voice was quiet, a bare whisper, with only his wife—they were married, Tom saw the rings—and Tom hearing it. "When we get home—"

And then the picture was taken, and they were leaving, and Tom did something on instinct, without thinking, the same mischief he did before, but this time, with someone he shouldn't mess with. But he didn't care, Gutsy didn't care, *Gutsy did what he wanted.* Gutsy grabbed Sam's flat-brimmed hat, fresh, and clean, in the red and black of the

Brawlers, and threw it as hard as he could down the concourse.

Fuck you, Sam.

Most people responded with laughter, and would humbly go retrieve their hat, usually with the help of the event staff. Gutsy's antics were typically harmless in the long run.

But Sam didn't respond with laughter. Sam responded with rage. He turned to face Gutsy, face to face, and Tom had to look up at his anger filled eyes.

"You motherfucker!" yelled Sam, bellowing it now, and he lunged at Tom, not going for the long neck, but for the head of Gutsy, because no one thought about the person inside. Everyone reacted to Gutsy as if he was a real creature.

Sam's big hands went to Gutsy's head, grabbing it, squeezing it, trying to take it off.

Tom struggled, putting his hands up to hold on to the head, so it wouldn't be removed in public. Shattering the illusion of Gutsy was one of the big no-no's, and he couldn't—

No.

Visions flashed through Tom's mind. Blood, death, chaos. His breath froze and his heart pumped, his mind filled with visions of death. Images of knives sliding into flesh, with blood pouring out. Clubs crushing skulls, the bones shattering, with brain matter leaking out of ears and eyes and nose. The sound of vertebrae shattering, of flesh being sliced. The sound of a death rattle reverberating through an empty alley as a man was killed, empty, and alone, a meaningless life ended brutally.

Not just any man dying. It was this man, Sam, repeatedly, his body being broken and destroyed in a thousand different ways. Tom saw it all, all through the red lens of

Gutsy's eyes, blood filling his vision.

And then Shannon and the event staff were pulling Sam off him, and security was there, three strong men, pulling Sam away, and Sam was yelling and ranting and cursing, the hundreds of people in the area all staring at him, all staring at Gutsy.

Gutsy's head was still on his shoulders, still firmly locked onto his head. He had held it on. Sam had only been there a second before they had grabbed him. They led him away to the exit, his wife Marcia following meekly behind.

Shannon was there, directly in front of him.

"You okay?" she asked, below her breath.

"I—I need a break," said Tom. The visions still lingered in front of his eyes. "Just a moment away from the crowd."

"Here alright?" asked Shannon. "I can shut it down if you want—"

"No," said Tom, he looked out, still a good dozen people in line. "They've been waiting for a while. Just five minutes, and then we can finish with everyone still in line."

He stood there, catching his breath. What was that? He shouldn't have taken that guy's hat, he knew he shouldn't have, but he couldn't stop himself. Couldn't stop himself from that small amount of retribution.

Don't blame yourself.

He shouldn't blame himself. That guy was a dick. Threw him out of the arena, maybe even banned him. It's what he deserved. But what were those visions? So awful. The thought of them made his stomach turn, but with every passing moment the visions lessened, and lessened, and then there was nothing left for him to latch onto. He could breathe again, and his heartbeat was back to normal. He gave Shannon the high sign, and she waved on the next group of people, who were a little afraid from what they saw. Tom did his best to entertain them.

*

The game started, but Tom's job didn't stop. He walked around the arena, through the upper and lower concourses. Gutsy would stop for selfies here, because the crowd would be much thinner. In between periods, when the people would use the break in the action to use the bathroom or get snacks would serve as chances for Gutsy to entertain the crowd still in their seats. As the memories of the visions faded, and the busyness of the night engaged Tom's attention, his earlier episode was forgotten. He moved around the arena and took pictures with fans. He did quick bits for the cameras during breaks and took a quick shot with Barbara and the PR team for one of the team's business partners.

It wasn't hard. He just played Gutsy. That was the beauty of Gutsy. He was expected to disrupt the normal flow of business, and so when he didn't do the normal, boring thing, it was perfectly acceptable. So when he tousled the well-kept hair of the multi-millionaire, and then pelvic thrusted behind him as he tried to make a serious speech for the camera, it was expected. Hell, it was encouraged.

"You do a great job," said the multi-millionaire, straightening his hair, and shaking Gutsy's hand, smiling, before walking away back to his luxury box.

Then the second intermission came, time for the one more extended bit they always do. These were really the only things they rehearsed. They had practiced it earlier today. It seemed simple.

Gutsy would be sitting in a seat, cartoonishly devouring a plate of hot dogs. Gutsy didn't have a working mouth, so he would mostly be destroying them and knocking them around on the people around him. But he'd play up how much he was enjoying the food.

Then, he would look over, see a person dressed in a hot dog outfit. Shannon will have changed out of her suit into the hot dog costume. They would engage in a short chase, and then he would rip the hot dog costume off, leaving Shannon in a black lycra bodysuit. Gutsy would shake the outfit triumphantly to the crowd, and Shannon would run off.

And it was going great. The arena cameras were trained on him as he threw hot dogs around, breaking them into little pieces. He did it for a solid thirty seconds, finally breaking the plate when there were no more pieces of hot dogs. And then he waited, and waited, and then craned Gutsy's head over to look at Shannon in a ridiculous hot dog costume.

And he timed it in his head, and went to go for her, to start their chase sequence, up and down the stairs, around a balcony, but then a group of three drunk fans surrounded him, all trying to get a picture, and they were right in the way, and they were standing on the stairs, and if he pushed through them, he'd probably kill them—

You're fucking up the timing!

His frustration grew to anger in a split second, and he wanted to push them, wanted to knock them down the fucking stairs, but then the picture was taken and they went back to their seats and he chased after Shannon, but that anger was still there, manifested in just a moment, and he felt all the energy he had built with the lead up to the bit gone. He finished it anyway, his heart pounding, and the crowd cheered, but something was missing, and if it wasn't for those fucking guys, it would have gone right—*Goddamnit, goddamnit!*

Take a breath, Tom.

The bit was over, and the third period was starting, and all eyes were off him. Shannon had run away, hiding in a corner of the concourse, and his rage was subsiding. He felt his hands shaking in the costume. What the hell had come over him?

He walked over to where Shannon waited.

"I need a break," he said. "I need to get out of the suit."

"We can call it," said Shannon. "Here." She pulled a card from inside the lycra suit and beeped open the door, and they went through, and soon they were back in the break room.

"Help," said Tom, and Shannon grabbed Gutsy's head, much like that dude Sam had earlier, and a brief glimpse of blood and chaos flashed through Tom's vision, and then the head was off, on the table in front of him, and he saw normal again. He sat down, exhausted.

"You okay?" Shannon asked.

Tom took a deep breath. "It was hard," he said.

"It's a tougher job than you think."

"I can see why people quit," said Tom. "It sneaks up on you."

"You did a good job out there," said Shannon. "Especially after that asshole tried to rip your head off."

"I know I shouldn't have messed with him, but you didn't

hear what he said to his wife."

"They talk like you're not even there," said Shannon. "I don't blame you for fucking with him. One of the perks of the job. You can fuck with assholes. Normally they don't attack Gutsy. They know they'll get kicked out."

"Douchebag deserved it," said Tom. He took a deep breath.

"You're not quitting on me, are you?"

"No," said Tom. "I need the money. Barely had the gas to make it to the arena today—"

"You need some cash?" she asked. "Until the first paycheck—"

"I'm not going to take your money, Shannon," he said. "I can get by."

"I know how it is," she said. "I bounced off five or six jobs until I found this one. If you need help, ask. I'll do what I can. We're all we have." She eyed him. "But I'll say this. You have what it takes. The last couple guys, they didn't. They floundered around in Gutsy. You're a natural. A few more times in the costume, and you'll be as good as me."

"I appreciate it," said Tom. "I know what to expect now, I guess."

"I'm going to change and head home," said Shannon. "Can I trust you to put up the suit by yourself?"

"Yeah, I can do it," said Tom.

"We have tomorrow off," said Shannon. "Home stand is a couple more games, and then the Brawlers take a road trip. Gives us a bit of a breather."

"That's good to hear," said Tom. "I think I need it." Shannon turned to leave. "Shannon—"

She turned back. "Yes?"

"When you're in the suit—?"

"When I'm in the suit, what?"

Tom thought back to the visions of red, almost all gone in his mind. The sudden rage. They dispersed.

"Nothing," said Tom. "It's nothing. I'll see you Saturday."

"See you," said Shannon, and she was gone, to change, to leave. Tom was left alone in the break room. Gutsy's head sat in front of him on the table.

Tom grabbed it, much like Sam did earlier. He squared the head, turned it, so his eyes stared right into Gutsy's. He looked for anything, anything behind those cartoonish, rage-filled eyes.

Nothing. Nothing there.

5

He was hungry, and the world was red.

That's all he knew, as he moved through it. The hunger dominated everything else. There was a well within him, so deep it could never be filled, but still it demanded it, and it needed blood.

That much was clear, in this hazy red world Tom found himself in. He swam in it, floated in it, enveloped by it. The red was everywhere, and everything. Inside that red was prey, soft creatures filled with blood and guts and pain, and the only way to fill that well was to squeeze them until nothing inside was left, drain them dry into the well.

He needed blood. He needed *chaos*. The blood could be measured, weighed, and quantified, along with the flesh, and muscle, and bone. The organs and viscera, too. All could be weighed and dumped into the well.

The chaos, there was no measuring tool on Earth that could put a number on that hell, the mixture of fear and pain and worry, sprung up in the wake of murder and death. Even so, it filled the well, filled it more than all the blood in the world, and with enough, the well would overflow.

The well *would* overflow.

Tom tried to focus, tried to collect his thoughts. He had fallen asleep, after fits and starts, and he had awoken in this red world. It was hard to piece together where he was. What he was. He couldn't see, see anything but the crimson that ebbed and flowed, the world outlined in degrees of claret. Everything was red, everything he touched, as he moved. Every breath breathed in red.

Then he recognized shapes. Pulled out images from the red, and he understood, or *began* to understand. He was moving, moving through the red. He saw buildings, streets, cars. As the Red shifted around him, he parsed the visual language, and saw the perspective. He was moving through a city.

But it wasn't smooth. He felt his vision jump, move between buildings, his perspective changing from low to high.

Then he saw the people, and his hunger struck him, hard. He needed to *kill*, demanded to *feed*, not just on their blood, but on their pain, on the chaos waves, the ripples of fear and worry that sprang out in the wake of destruction. He *required it*. He had desired nothing more in his entire life, and now he understood, understood the Red, as he sorted prey, searching for a weak body, a fragile shell, a small, struggling creature he could separate from the pack, and destroy, rip out their throat, and drain their innards, and swallow them whole.

And he saw them. He saw one here, one there, floating through the Red, down a city street, alone, solitary. He could kill them. Drive them down an alley, like a gazelle, and rip out its throat like a lion.

But no, no, despite all that hunger, there was an even deeper need, nested inside that urge.

Vengeance.

Rage simmered inside, glowing bright red within that hunger, and he knew, somehow, that feeding that vengeance, claiming that revenge would fill the well, fill it faster still. And he needed it filled, just like he needed to feed.

But where was his target? Where was his *nemesis*?

They were here, he knew they were. They had touched, and he had marked them in that instance, and he could follow them anywhere.

They were here, in the area still.

He swam through the Red, appearing at will, in the spaces that no one looked, and disappeared at the merest glance, at any prey noticing him out of the corner of his eye, any sense of the red lurking in the corner.

Glasses clinked and his vision in the Red changed again, and he saw a bar, crowded with prey, loaded with the bags of blood and flesh. But one in particular was what he hunted, and he saw him there, sitting at the bar, empty glasses in front of him. He was alone.

Perfect.

Someone at a table cast their glance in his direction and he appeared in another hollow, in one of the thousand spaces of vacuum, where no eyes looked. No matter your size, there was always a place no one was watching.

As he spent more time in the Red, Tom understood, even as his mind struggled with where he was, with *what* he was. Was this real? Or was he—

But the hunger pushed away all thought. The need drove away any logic, and all he wanted was to feed. To feed on his target, and he waited, surely, he could wait forever, and then his target shifted in the moving fluids of the Red, and put down his drink, and stumbled out of the bar. He wandered down the street, and Tom followed, moving through the Red, without thought, appearing where he needed to be.

The man stumbled down the street, his footsteps scattered. A few people passed him, avoiding him.

He yelled into the night air, words that were garbled, distorted in the Red. All sound was, but as time went on, Tom listened, and he could parse the words, eventually.

"I've been a fan my whole life!" yelled the man. "Those sons of bitches!" He shouted into the air, steam coming out with every breath, heat rising off him in the cold. Tom didn't feel cold, not in the Red. He felt warm, maybe even hot, a heat rising in his chest, the rage building. This was his target, his prey, his gazelle, and he would drive him off, down and away, and he would sink his teeth in.

"You can't treat me that way," said the prey. The words were becoming softer, mumbled beneath his breath, and Tom stopped listening. There was only the hunt. Only instinct, and then blood, and then death. He would fill the well.

He was behind him, lurking, looking down on him, on the softness of his flesh. His stomach didn't growl, he had no stomach, but the need, the same need doubled, and then tripled, brought on by his closeness to his prey.

What is this, what is happening, is this real—

The thoughts intruded, but the need drowned them out, snuffed them, suffocated them, and he hunted. The gazelle turned, hearing Tom behind him, but then he was gone in an instant, travel instantaneous in the Red, and the man turned, and he moved again, behind him.

The prey stood at an alleyway, the sidewalk opening up to the slim space between buildings, a dumpster halfway down. Tom reached out in the Red, and moved the suspension, moved the Red, and it caressed the back of the man's head, a cloud of crimson splashing him. He barely reacted, the caress too subtle for him to understand drunk.

"Iss—" started the man, gibberish coming from his mouth. "—take a leak," he finished, and walked down the alley, his feet catching him from falling. He moved slowly, and Tom moved behind him through the Red, silently. He loomed behind him, but the prey didn't look back, not anymore. He stumbled past the dumpster, ducking behind it to pee.

His hunger strained inside, and Tom felt like he would burst, it hurt so bad, he'd never been this hungry, a yearning, a need for something that had no name, and pallets were stacked next to the dumpster. A half dozen, as tall as he was. They would do, they would do. He wrapped a powerful hand around one of the pieces of wood, and it moved easily, covered in jagged wood and sharp nails. He lifted it, with one hand, and it made a noise, but it was too late for his prey, and he brought it down, as hard as he could, a swift motion—

Tom gasped, his eyes open in the dark, dim light of his bedroom. He blinked, but there was no Red, there was no red. He rubbed his eyes, and looked at the clock. It was 5 AM, he'd only been asleep for a few hours.

What was that nightmare? He sat up, fear still gripping his heart—

—*no, not fear. Need.*

But it was already slipping away. The finer details washed away, but Tom didn't forget it all. He couldn't forget the Red.

*

"Have you ever had nightmares after you've worn the suit?" he asked. He sat across from Shannon. It was the next home game, two days later. Tom had spent those two days relaxing and organizing his finances. Planning out his paychecks, and knowing when to pay off his back rent, and inevitable car repairs, and how to eat on fifteen dollars a week.

He'd also spent it trying to forget the weird nightmare that, no matter what he did, wouldn't vanish from his mind. He'd forgotten most of the minor details, but he didn't forget the Red, or the terrible need deep inside that called for blood and chaos.

He couldn't forget it, and he couldn't overlook the connections to wearing the Gutsy suit. Looking through and seeing only red.

Shannon reacted, looking at him suddenly, her eyes jumping away from her phone. "What did you say?"

"Have you ever had nightmares after being Gutsy?" asked Tom. "I had terrible, just terrible, nightmares the other night."

Shannon stared at him for a long second, before looking back at her phone. "What kind of nightmares?"

"It's hard to describe," said Tom. "I can't remember it all. I just remember—I remember red. I remember the whole world being red. And feeling so hungry. But hungry isn't the right word. It was just this need. I can't describe it."

"Do you remember anything else?"

"I remember anger," said Tom. "No, not anger. Rage. And—" Tom closed his eyes. "—hunting."

"Hunting?" asked Shannon. She stared at him again.

"Yes," said Tom. "I don't remember the details." He opened his eyes, and Shannon looked away again, back at her phone. "The exact thing doesn't matter. It's more wondering if you've had any nightmares after wearing the suit."

"No, never," said Shannon, quickly, staring at her phone. "I'm usually so tired after games that I sleep like the dead. No dreams or nightmares."

"That makes sense."

"Listen, it was your first time, and that dude attacked you, remember? That's a traumatic experience. Not everyone is going to react the same way. Nightmares are just the way your body deals with trauma, sometimes."

"Do you have a lot of nightmares?"

Shannon looked up at him again. "I—I used to. But not anymore. But I wouldn't worry about it. I'm sure once you're used to wearing the suit, your mind will react differently."

"I hope so," said Tom. "I don't think I could take something like that every night. I might lose my mind."

Shannon said nothing, still looking at her phone. They were still hours away from game time.

"What bit are we doing tonight?"

"Oh, we should probably do a new one. Keep expanding your repertoire. Want to practice it?"

"Sure," said Tom. "You're wearing the suit tonight, right?"

"Yeah, that was the plan," said Shannon. "Unless you want the time in it."

"No, no," said Tom. "I'm happy just being a handler tonight."

"Fine with me," said Shannon. "Remember, one more game, then they have a road trip."

"Do we just sit at home?" asked Tom.

"Depends," said Shannon. "A lot of time, the PR team will have lined up business opps with Gutsy appearances. I'll talk to Barbara later, and I'll let you know." Shannon shoved her phone into her pocket.

"Shit, I forgot to tell you. The holiday party is tomorrow night."

"Do I have to go?" asked Tom.

"You don't *have* to," said Shannon. "But it'd look better if you did. And it's free food and drinks."

"Now you're speaking my language," said Tom. "I'm there."

"I'll forward you the email," said Shannon. "You should already be on the list." She tapped at her phone for a second. "There, you should have the email. Let's go practice. Oh, and Skates said his wife made some extra cookies. She always makes a million of them. If we're lucky, we might have some goody bags to take home."

Tom smiled. Hard to be upset about cookies.

Nevertheless, he was glad Shannon was wearing the suit tonight.

6

"Man, this is fancy," said Tom.

"The Altmans go all out for their holiday parties," said Shannon. "They're billionaires. This is chump change to them." They sat at a big, round table, covered in a white tablecloth, with a bright angelic centerpiece in the middle of the table. The Altmans were the owners of the Brawlers, along with a bunch of other industry in the city. Tom had seen them across the room, talking to a bunch of the players. They were all dressed up in suits and ties. He felt kind of schlubby, wearing a button-down shirt and his fanciest pair of blue jeans.

"The food is great," said Tom. He had loaded up a plate with a selection of everything, even the stuff he normally wouldn't get. His stomach growled. He was hungry. He hadn't eaten yet today. Partially because he knew he'd be getting free food tonight, plus it would help stretch his food budget further.

"You know you're allowed to go back for more, right?" asked Shannon. Her own plate was a little more modest. She only drank water, while Tom had grabbed a free beer. He'd never been anywhere with an open bar.

"I know," said Tom. "I'm just starving. Can I—can I just go ahead and eat?"

"What are you waiting for, a toast?"

"I've never been to anything like this before," said Tom. "Most of the holiday parties I've been to have in somebody's parent's house."

"Eat," said Shannon. "They'll have a toast in a little while, probably, but they don't expect you to wait." Tom didn't stand on ceremony, and ate his dinner. It tasted great, and after a few minutes, the gnawing hunger inside him subsided. He wondered if he could find a way to take some home.

"Thanks for hanging with me," said Tom. "I don't really know anyone else here."

"You know Skates," said Shannon. "Beverly is here— somewhere." There were hundreds of people milling around. Beverly was an usher in the arena, who worked with PR to arrange certain areas for their skits. She was a pleasant old lady who Tom liked. Still, he didn't know what the hell they would talk about if they ate dinner together.

"I mean, our age," said Tom.

"Cloudy is our age," said Shannon.

"Cloudy is built like a tree trunk."

"Still, he's our age," said Shannon. "Most hockey players don't make it that long."

"Jeez," said Tom. "I suddenly feel old."

"Just a fact of life," said Shannon. "Hockey players peak early. It's a rough sport."

"I still don't really know all the rules."

Shannon sighed. "It's really not complicated."

"I still don't understand what icing is."

"We'll watch a game together sometime, and I'll go over the rules. You should really know them. You work for a hockey team."

"Yeah, and I used to work for Disney. Doesn't mean I know how Space Mountain works," said Tom. "Do you know all the rules?"

"Well, yeah," said Shannon. "I've been a Brawlers fan my whole life."

"Oh, I didn't realize," said Tom. "I thought you just needed a job."

"I mean, I wasn't lying," said Shannon. "I did, desperately. But if you fill your cover letter with details about how important the team is to you, you're more likely to be hired for a role that is technically PR. Before Gutsy showed up, I mostly just worked as a assistant to Barbara."

"Wait, yeah, that's a good question—who was the Brawler's mascot before Gutsy?"

"We didn't have one," said Shannon.

"There are teams without mascots?" asked Tom.

"Of course," said Shannon. "There's a bunch of them. But I think the Brawlers PR team saw an opportunity and jumped on it. And thus, Gutsy was born."

"Wait, so you've been Gutsy this entire time?"

"Yeah, kind of," said Shannon. "I mean, other people have been in and out, but I've always been a part of the team."

"You're responsible for him then," said Tom. "For like, all that viral success. That's awesome."

"Believe me, I know," said Shannon. "I wish I got paid like it."

"You should get an ownership claim, or something," said Tom. "It's your acting that put him on the map."

"They've given me raises, so it's hard for me to complain," said Shannon. "But it's out of my control. It was part of the contract I signed. And now the genie is out of the bottle. Hard to put it back in."

"That sucks," said Tom.

"Hey, at least I can pay my bills, and the team has a 401k program. We have health insurance. More than a lot of people can say."

Tom sighed and took a long swig of beer. "Do you ever feel guilty?"

"Guilty?" she asked. "For what?"

"For living," said Tom. "For being able to pay your bills."

"No," said Shannon. "I didn't make the rules for the world. I only live in it. When I see someone who needs help, I try and help. But I'm one person."

"You're right," said Tom. "You think they'll let us take food home with us?"

"I think there's to-go boxes up there. Or if you ask one of the caterers, they'll probably make you a plate. Just lie and say it's for your girlfriend who couldn't make it."

The night wound on, with the crowd reaching critical mass as most of the guests were there, the huge banquet hall filling with noise, between the guests and the live band. Some people even found the dance floor. Shannon introduced Tom to any people she knew, and Tom did his best to match names to faces, for later. He tried to think professionally. Maybe he didn't want to play Gutsy for the rest of his life. If he wanted to get promoted, he'd need to network.

John Altman made a speech, discussing the success of the team, and how it wouldn't be possible without all of them, and Tom tried to pay attention, but he couldn't, instead focusing his attention on the fancy donut the catering had provided, with cosmic swirl icing. He ate one, and then immediately got a second. Shannon had been right, because he'd asked a caterer nicely for leftovers and they had handed him a large takeout container, which he had filled to the brim.

After Altman's speech, the crowd thinned. It was still relatively early on a Friday night, and most of the hockey players were the first to go, along with the Altmans and other minority owners. The richest retreated to their homes, or to their expensive night clubs, leaving the low and mid-level employees to enjoy the end of the holiday party.

Tom sat alone at their table, everyone else already left or out mingling. Shannon was dancing, and Tom had thought to join her, but he was just too damn tired, and had eaten too much. He had caught sight of the Gutsy cardboard stand-up that served as a stand in at the party, and the color red had flashed through his mind.

"You doing alright, Tommers?" asked a voice, and Tom looked up, and it was Cloudy, in a suit, his tie untied, strung around his neck. He sat down next to him, his thick legs straining at his slacks. Cloudy had settled on Tommers for his nickname, and while not the best, it was authentic. Shannon had informed him he'd gotten lucky. It could have been a lot worse.

"Yeah, I think I ate too much," said Tom.

"Chow is good, huh?" asked Cloudy. "I get so used to these things, you can forget how lucky we are."

"It's too good," said Tom. "My stomach is going to hate me in the morning."

"I think you'll make it," said Cloudy. "You're a Brawler. You're tough."

"Yeah, I guess so," said Tom. "I think you're the only player still here."

"There's still a couple left," said Cloudy. "I think Davo is still here. But mostly just the old-timers. Most of the kids don't want to stick around for longer than they have to. And I get it. I didn't want to either, when I was younger. How you like the job so far?"

"It's hard, to be honest," said Tom. "Especially being in the suit. It's a lot of work, and you have to be entertaining, and on your feet, and it's hard to see—" He looked at Cloudy. "—I'm not meaning to complain. I've had a lot worse jobs."

"No, I get it," said Cloudy. "I could never do that job. All I've ever known is hockey. But talking to Skates, and Woody, they really like you. Skates would never tell you that in a million years, so I'll tell you for him."

"Well, I appreciate that," said Tom. "I've only been here for a week or so—"

"You didn't grow up with it, but I wasn't lying about being family," said Cloudy. "I've been a Brawler my entire career, and the way it's looking, I'll retire one, too. And I wear the C, at least for now. So I look out for everyone."

"For captain, right?"

Cloudy chuckled. "Yeah," he said. "Least, that's what my dad always told me. Captains look out for everyone. You're a Brawler, even if you only come out on the ice to make people laugh." He paused, looked around, and saw they were still mostly alone. "Listen, I was talking to Skates—"

"And?" asked Tom. What was going on?

"And he mentioned you were having some money trouble," said Cloudy. Cloudy reached into his inner coat pocket and pulled out an envelope, and handed it over, looking into Tom's eyes. Tom took it silently, eyeing the envelope. He peeked inside. It was filled to the brim with one hundred-dollar bills.

"Holy shit," said Tom. He immediately tried to hand it back. "I can't take this, Cloudy. This must be at least five thousand dollars."

"It's ten K," said Cloudy. "All the players chipped in."

"I can't accept this," said Tom, still holding it out to Cloudy. "I've only worked here a week."

"Doesn't matter," he said. "Take the envelope, close it, and shove it in your front pocket. Pay your bills. Get your car fixed. Buy yourself some groceries."

"I don't know what to say," said Tom.

"You don't have to say anything," said Cloudy. "Happy holidays. I'll see you tomorrow." And then Cloudy stood up, patted him on the shoulder, and walked back into the crowd. Tom stared at the envelope. He couldn't believe it, and the immense weight of his back rent, and his broken-down car, and his empty fridge, it all evaporated, and he shut the envelope closed, and shoved it into his front pocket, bulging now.

He suddenly felt very vulnerable, with that incredible amount of money in his pocket.

"God almighty, I hate these things," said a voice, one

Tom recognized. It was Skates, who sat down next to him, where Cloudy had just departed.

"You don't have to come," said Tom.

"No, but where else do I get free beer?" asked Skates. "You don't look a gift horse in the mouth. Or an open bar in the tab."

"Touche," said Tom. Skates carried a beer, but Tom had no idea how much Skates had drank. He looked the same as always. Even wearing a Brawlers polo, like he wore at the stadium.

"Saw you talking to Cloudy," said Skates.

"Yeah," said Tom. "He—"

"He's a good fella," said Skates. "Despite all the talk about family, there's a lot of jerk-offs in hockey. Not Cloudy. He's one of the good ones."

"Can't argue with that," said Tom, feeling the wad of cash in his pocket.

"Think you'll be sticking around with us?" asked Skates.

"I think so," said Tom. "I mean, I can't predict the future."

"No one can," said Skates. "If I could, my life sure as hell would be different."

"How so?"

"Well, for starters, I would have dodged that cheapshottin' motherfucker Dwayne Hartford who took out my knee in '73." He patted his left knee. The limp.

"It's not just a nickname," said Tom.

"I was like the wind," said Skates. "My hands were only okay, but that didn't matter. No one could catch me. But Dwayne's coach told him to take me out, and that's what he did. Never was the same after that. Our enforcer, Blocks, he beat the shit out of Dwayne. Didn't fix my knee, though.

Maybe if it had happened today, they could have fixed me. But not then."

"Sorry to hear that," said Tom. "I didn't realize."

"It's alright, kid," said Skates. "When I've got some drink in me, I get mopey. Shouldn't, though. I've had it good. How many people get to spend their entire life around something they love?" Skates stared at him. "Not many, that's how many. Not many. Think I'm gonna go home, kid. Encourage you to do the same. Be careful out there. Don't get murdered, you know."

"Murdered? What?" asked Tom.

"You don't watch the news, kid?" asked Skates. "It's all they've talked about for weeks now. Bunch of random people killed throughout the city. Unpredictable. They say it's a serial killer."

"How do they know that?" asked Tom.

"Oh, I don't know," said Skates. "News always lies, anyway. Just be careful. I'll see ya tomorrow."

7

Tom had deposited the cash in his bank account that night, racing to an ATM, feeling paranoid the whole time. But as soon as the cash hit his account, he paid off his bills and wrote a check for his back rent. His car would have to wait until a day off.

Then why did he feel so anxious? Why did his stomach hurt so much? He'd had a tension in him, impossible to ignore, but one he had to live with, knowing he owed so much money, a sword of Damocles hanging over his head.

But now he was free, thanks to Cloudy and the rest of the players. He'd have to thank them, even if it was just a card.

But the worry in his gut didn't go away, and as he arrived at the arena, he realized what it was, realized that he'd been pushing away the thoughts that had lurked in his mind.

The feelings of rage that had overcome him. The visions of brutal death and murder. And the nightmare. The Red.

He had forced them away, because they didn't make any logical sense. But they were there anyway, and his guts still ached at the thought of putting the suit on again, and possibly invoking those same feelings.

But he forced that away too. Because the thought was crazy. It was just a costume. Shannon wore it, and she was fine. She didn't have nightmares. She didn't almost lose control when she was in the suit. He'd served as handler for her twice now, and both times had gone perfectly fine.

It was just nerves. Just inexperience. Tom swallowed those feelings down and compressed them into his stomach, into a tight little ball.

He got to the arena early. He had brought a book this time, even as Shannon sat there and stared at her phone. He read, and waited for showtime.

Well, tried to read. He'd brought the third book in a fantasy series he'd recently started, and that he'd really liked, but as he read, his eyes danced over the page, over words, but nothing sunk in. He found himself re-reading pages, hell, whole chapters, because none of it was staying with him.

After a while, he put the book back in his locker and took a walk around the arena, to get some fresh air, to calm himself down. The arena was cool already, and he watched them lay down the ice, a process he'd never seen before.

But still, his anxiety remained, and nothing he did could keep his mind off the Red. Before he knew it, it was time to rehearse with Shannon, a new bit they would do tonight, and then the players were practicing, out on the ice, and then more staff arrived, and then the VIPs, and then it was time for him to put on the suit, and he dreaded it, nothing he could do or think would stop him from dreading it, but Gutsy's eyes stared directly at him, once again, empty, nothing but the empty cartoon rage and the tufted red eyebrows.

"You ready?" asked Shannon. Tom nodded, even though he wasn't ready, but if he didn't do it now, he would never do it, and then the head was on him, shifting around on his skull, and then the foam seated correctly and he looked out through the red and everything felt fine again.

Why were you so worried?

It was easy, and any awkwardness he remembered in the suit from the last time he wore it washed away in a flood of ambrosia. It felt good in the suit. Better than good. It felt like a second skin. The suit fit him better, somehow, and he was even sweating less.

All the anxiety, all the worry, it was gone.

"You good?" asked Shannon, looking into his eyeholes.

"Yeah, I'm good," said Tom. And he meant it. Shannon wore her suit, and he followed her out into the photo op area. The line was long again, it was always long, everyone loved Gutsy.

The interactions felt more natural this time, and he slipped right back into Gutsy's behavior. He taunted people, did the same miming gags, and when in doubt, did pelvic thrusting, which made the crowd cheer every single time. And sure, there were the same amount of slightly sloppy drunk people, and babies and children who were terrified of him, but there weren't any possessive fans who screamed expletives or whispered threats to their wife. Everything went well, and the game started, and they moved onto his crowd work.

See? You were worried about nothing.

And he had been. Because Shannon had been completely right. It was all just stress from being attacked. It had fucked him up. Hell, now that he had health insurance, he could even see a therapist, something he'd wanted to do for a while, but felt like a pipe dream. Now, it was possible.

The crowd work went well, and the night was moving fast. Before he realized it, it was the second intermission, and time for their extended bit. This time, they'd be on the ice.

Shannon was playing the part of an ordinary fan this time. They didn't always use plants, but whenever the situation had the barest chance of becoming litigious, they used one of them. Season ticket holders might become aware, eventually, but even they rarely paid close attention to who was who.

They stood on the ice, something they'd practiced earlier today. Tom had walked on frozen sidewalks before. You took small steps, and shuffled like a penguin, and generally, you wouldn't eat shit. But he had never done it in a mascot outfit, so he'd practiced in the oversized feet of Gutsy throughout the week. It wasn't the end of the world if he fell. It was ice. Hockey players fell down all the time.

Amy stood on the ice with them. Amy did it in high heels, without even a stumble. Tom didn't know how. She stood next to Shannon.

"We have a lucky contestant here today. What's your name?"

"Jennifer!" yelled Shannon, mustering more excitement than Tom had seen her use in the week plus he'd known her.

"Well, Jennifer, are you ready for today's game?"

"Yes!" said Jennifer. "I love games!"

"That's great news," said Amy. "Because today, you're playing t-shirt cannon duel!" The crowd cheered at the sound of it, because Gutsy pulled up a t-shirt cannon from one of the two barrels that stood on the ice. The cannon had been tucked inside the barrel, the barrel otherwise filled with t-shirts. Amy and Shannon stood near the other.

"What—what's that?" asked Shannon.

"You and Gutsy will wait until the count of three, and then you'll fire your t-shirt cannons at each other. The first to land a hit will be declared the winner!"

"What do I get if I win?" asked Shannon.

"A free Brawlers t-shirt!" yelled Amy.

"And if I lose?" asked Shannon.

"A free Brawlers t-shirt!" yelled Amy. "Alright, Jennifer. Grab your cannon from inside the barrel, and stand right next to it." Amy walked as she talked, moving quickly in her high heels. Soon, she was off the ice.

"Okay, on three. One, two—" and then before she could say three, Gutsy took the cannon out of the barrel and fired it at Shannon. The crowd roared.

The bit was simple and required almost no rehearsal. Moving around on the ice in the suit was the trickier thing. But Tom had the bit in his mind, and how it would go. He knew it. He knew what he was supposed to do.

He didn't know what happened, and why he didn't follow the script.

He missed his first shot. That part was supposed to happen. Shannon drew her cannon and fired at him, and missed as well. That was also supposed to happen. They would build suspense, missing their first few shots, and then finally, Shannon would land one, but Gutsy obviously wouldn't give up, and he would keep firing, missing, and then a couple security staff would come and drag him away.

"Aim low," Shannon had said earlier that day. "The cannons won't kill anyone, but if they clock me, or you, in the head, they definitely could knock you out. And if you smash your head on the ice, it could be real bad. I'll be wearing a helmet, but even then, aim low. If you accidentally hit me in the leg or the butt, it'll sting a little, but it won't kill me. Understand?"

He did. He did understand. But his hands in the Gutsy suit strayed higher. Tom tried to keep his aim low, but they shot higher anyway, the first shot that missed whizzing by Shannon's head.

The cannon in his arms, the vision of the rolled t-shirt hitting Shannon, and cartoonishly snapping her head back, like JFK in Dealey Plaza, filled his mind. But moment by moment, it got bloodier, more violent.

Shannon looked alarmed, but continued with the bit, missing her shot low. Tom aimed and fired again, and this shot went high too, but Shannon dodged it again, her eyes screaming at him to aim lower.

The vision filled his mind this time, taking control of him. This time it hit her in the throat, and collapsed her windpipe. She would collapse on the ice, choking to death, suffocating.

She fired this time, and this time she aimed for center mass. It would hit him, and then they could wrap up the bit.

But Tom dodged the fire, moving his body suddenly to the side, an agility he was surprised he had in the bulky suit. He hadn't been hit, and so the duel went on, and he fired again, a third shot, and this narrowly missed Shannon's head.

Another vision, another glimpse of Shannon dying grotesquely, the t-shirt punching a hole right through her skull, something impossible, but he saw it, her skull shattering, her brains popping out of the back of her head.

A dissonance was in him, the awful recognition of these terrible visions, of murder and death, and he hated it, and he couldn't stop it. But the other existed as well. The Red existed.

It wanted death. It lingered in that feeling.

He didn't know what was happening. He couldn't drop the gun, he couldn't aim lower. His hands had a mind of their own, and Shannon didn't fire again, instead charging him. He was still reloading his cannon and she hit him in the torso, with just enough force for them to gently fall over, and she pulled the gun away from his hands with a sudden yank.

Tom lost all sense of where he was. He'd never been inside the suit on the ground, and it was much like being a turtle. He couldn't really move. Shannon pushed herself off him, and then stood up, threw his cannon in the barrel, and shot him in the leg with hers.

Motherfucker!

It hurt like hell, but it worked, snapping him out of the fugue state, the red visions disappearing from behind his eyes.

"We have a winner!" yelled Amy. Shannon walked off the ice, not looking back.

"Where's my t-shirt?" asked Shannon, and the crowd yelled as she took it and raised her hands on the side of the ice. Moments later, the security came out and helped him to his feet, and attendants removed the barrels and the t-shirt cannons.

Tom wandered off the ice and through the door to the innards of the arena.

"What the fuck was that, Tom?" asked Shannon.

"Please help me get the head off," said Tom.

"No, you tell me why the fuck you were aiming for my head. You knew the bit—"

"I'm sorry, Shannon, I am," said Tom. He couldn't breathe, suddenly, his heart beating hard in his chest. His hands were shaking. "Please, get this head off me."

Shannon stared at him for a long second, her eyes still angry, and then she relented, and pulled the head off, sticking at first, for a long moment, and then sliding off him.

He saw the world in normal colors again, and he took a deep breath.

They were alone in the corridor. He leaned back against the concrete wall.

"I don't know what happened. I know that's a shit excuse, but my hands weren't doing what I told them. I kept seeing things, I don't know, visions or something, and my hands—"

Tom looked into Shannon's eyes, expecting anger, but now saw fear.

"What visions?"

Tom took a deep breath. "Awful stuff, I don't know—you dying, in bad ways. It was ridiculous. The t-shirt cannon blowing a hole in you. Which isn't how it would work. But that's what I saw. And I felt like I don't know—you ever play D&D?"

"Dungeons and Dragons?" she asked. "What the hell—"

"Yes or no?"

"Yes, I've played."

"I felt like a raging barbarian, if that makes any sense," said Tom. "Like my vision was just filled with blood, or something. It doesn't make any sense. It's not the first time it's happened in the suit. I was doing completely fine today, until I got that cannon in my hand, and then a switch flipped or something."

Shannon stared at him, and then away, and then back at him. She took a breath. "I think you've been in the suit too long."

"I don't—"

"Do you feel better now?"

"Yes, much better," he said. "I can breathe again."

"Breathing is important," she said. "We don't have another home game for ten days. I know we have an off-site event coming up, but other than that, we mostly have the time off. I think that dude fucking with you—"

"I don't think it was that—"

"Tom," she said. "We're done for the night, anyway. I believe you when you say you didn't mean to aim for me. Take a breather, and we can talk about it later, when both of us aren't so tired or fired up. Okay?"

Tom looked at her. She was trying to stay calm. He *had* just tried to shoot her in the face.

"Okay," he said. "I'll change."

"You can go home," said Shannon. "I'll close everything up. Get some sleep."

Tom changed, opting not to take a shower there. He drove home, his car making it back, despite running low on brake fluid again. He'd get that fixed.

He turned up the radio, trying to blast away those errant thoughts, the visions of Shannon dying in terrible ways, but the sound did nothing, and he eventually turned the music off completely, instead letting the silence envelop him.

Tom still needed to shower, but instead, he collapsed in bed once he got home. His body was drained, empty, exhausted.

But once in bed, he couldn't sleep. He tossed and turned, red behind his eyes whenever he closed them. He wanted nothing more than sleep.

But something burned inside, an urge he couldn't extinguish. He wanted it, he needed it, and he didn't know what it was. It wasn't hunger, and it wasn't sex.

Then he realized. His body craved the suit. He needed to be Gutsy again.

8

Tom's weariness won out over his errant thoughts, over his body's urges. He fell asleep.

The Red waited for him there.

No, no, please, not again—

The dissonance remained, his conscious mind active still somewhere in this nightmare, but it was pushed aside, barreled through by the hunger, the desperate, clawing, aching need to feed. It shoved it, forced it down and back and held down his thoughts while he remained a passive observer.

No, not an observer. A passenger.

The world was red again, that much was true. He moved through a variety of reds, of soft pinks to dark crimson, the whole world bathed in claret. There was less waiting now, and within moments he saw the distinctive shapes, he saw the world through different eyes. And he saw prey.

Prey was the darkest of reds, a bold, dark crimson, a soft bag of flesh filled with heat and blood. They were everywhere, streaming from place to place. They crossed the street, they moved between bars, they weaved with their friends from corner to corner, moving onto the next place. All of them targets, and the urge inside to hunt, to kill, rose, and rose, desperate as they passed, and he smelled them.

No, it wasn't smell. It was something else, a sense that Tom had no word for, a sense for their capability of fear and loss and pain and the capacity for chaos. It wasn't a sense a human possessed, and Tom couldn't name it, not even after reading hundreds of the greatest works of the canon, not after his degree in literature, because this word didn't exist in any human language. But he knew it now, and he *felt* it.

He sensed who would hurt the most. He felt whose death would cause the biggest splash.

He knew how to cause the most pain.

He moved, slowly, in no rush, he'd been around a long time, but the hunger was real, but he couldn't make a mistake. Still, when someone saw him, when they caught a glimpse of red out of the corner of their eye, he vanished, melding with the shadows, appearing out of view. The best predator knew when it was seen.

Tom's perspective changed, over and over, peering at the crowds of targets, looking for the darkest red. But not only the darkest red. But someone vulnerable. A limping wildebeest, that could be culled from its pack. Left behind for only a moment, but a moment was all he would need.

He scanned, scanned—

No, stop this, please don't—

The desperate hunger pushed down Tom's dissent again, pushed it down harder, and then held him there, pinned against the walls of this space, whatever it was. It needed to feed, and it would hear no resistance, not from within.

He scanned, and he spotted a target, dark red, an incredible capacity for pain, and anguish, and chaos, and—

She was bending down, trying to fix her heel. It had gotten wedged in a hole in the sidewalk, and she hadn't been alone, she'd been with a cadre of friends, all half-drunk or more, crawling from one bar to another, it was her friend's birthday, she had wanted to do the pub crawl, but they wanted to get inside, she was meeting a guy here—

The target yanked at her heel, and he felt no eyes on him as he appeared behind her. She pulled at her shoe, and it came free, and she stood up to feel an impossibly strong hand close around her throat, and she tried to scream, but he squeezed, and nothing came out.

He lifted her off the ground and carried her into the adjacent alley, dirty, smelly, and empty. Eyes would have seen them on the street, and he couldn't move with them both.

She struggled in his grasp, and—

And so did Tom inside. He summoned a strength and shoved away from whatever held him down inside this thing, and—

And he let go of her, and she fell, and grunted, and then pushed to her feet, and ran, yelling, but he moved, moved only like he could, and he waited for her, and Tom felt a terrible push inside, in whatever this dream state was, and he appeared in front of the prey, and then Tom was awake.

His phone rang, vibrating on his nightstand. He looked at the clock. It was 5:30.

Tom coughed, hard, his mind still foggy and shaken from whatever the hell dream he had, another nightmare in the Red, and he was already losing details, he'd been hunting some poor woman—

He blinked hard, coughed again, and then grabbed his phone, hastily pulling out the charging cable, and looked at it in the darkness. It was his mom, and panic rose again inside him, *oh no, something happened*—

He answered.

"Mom?" he asked, his voice creeping out. "What's wrong?"

His mother's warm voice greeted him from the other side. "Oh, thank God, you're okay."

"Well, yeah, I guess," said Tom. "I'm awake. It's so early. Why are you calling?"

"I'm sorry, Tommy," she said. She always called him Tommy, even though he stopped going by it before he even hit puberty. "You know me, I never sleep anymore, and I was awake. I saw the news, and I knew it was crazy, I knew I shouldn't call, but I suddenly got a feeling, you know. I can't explain it. I think it's a mom thing. You just have that connection with your children. And I felt something from you, something bad, and I couldn't dismiss it. I knew you'd be sleeping, but I don't think I'd be able to live with myself if I didn't at least call—"

"Mom, slow down," said Tom. He sat up and swung his feet over to the side of the bed. He set them down on the floor. "What are you talking about? What news?"

"There was another one, Tommy," she said. "That's two in a week. And with you working at the arena now, I was worried. Maybe you went out after the game, and they didn't release any details, and I was so worried—"

"Two in a week? Two what?" asked Tom.

"Oh, Tommy, don't you watch the news?"

"No, not really," said Tom. "I've been busy, and most of it is just sensationalist garbage to frighten you—"

"Two dead people, Tommy," said his mom. "They think it's the same killer, picking back up. They can't be sure, though. They don't release all the details on the news anyway. But I couldn't get the idea out of my mind. There was a new one, early this morning. They just reported it."

"I'm fine, Mom," said Tom. "I came home straight from work and crashed. My days of bar-hopping are behind me."

"I'm so relieved," she said. "I'm sorry for waking you up. Like I said—I had this terrible feeling in my gut. A mother, she knows things."

"It's alright, Mom," he said. "Everything's fine—can I go back to sleep?"

"Oh, yes, of course. I'm so glad you're alright. I'll let you go back to bed. Bye, honey, I love you."

"I love you, too," said Tom, and ended the call, putting the phone back on his nightstand. He took a deep breath, and let it out, and swung his feet back onto the bed, laying down.

His heart still raced from the ending of his nightmare, of the phone call waking him up. He took deep breaths, calming himself down, his mind still foggy. His mom worried too much, he had told her she should look into anxiety medication, it would probably help, don't know why she was worried he'd be murdered—

Wait.

The fog lifted out of his mind, and the pieces clicked into

place, obvious now. A murder, early this morning, near the arena. His dream echoed through his mind, all the remaining pieces in clear focus. He had hunted, in his nightmare. He had moved through the Red, and dragged a woman into an alley, as Tom pulled the foggy pieces of the dream from the fog, into the light.

His stomach began to ache—

Oh God, no, no, it's impossible—

Slow down, Tom. Slow down. Take a breath. Think this through.

Tom took a deep breath, and then another. He pushed himself out of bed, to his small desk in the corner, to his laptop, the home of his half-written novels and abandoned screenplays. He sat down and flipped it open, booting it up, and opening his browser.

He went to the local news station, and it couldn't be missed, it was a big headline

Another murder, body ripped apart

Tom clicked on it, opening up the news brief. It had been posted only an hour ago, and there were still scant details. The murder had taken place early this morning, perhaps even late last night. The body had been torn apart. He scanned the article for information, but there was nothing else released, not yet.

But there was a second murder, his mother had said. The second in a week, and sure enough, he scrolled to the bottom of the piece and there were links, the first being the news story for the last killing, a few days prior.

Tom clicked on it, and the browser worked, the page loading. The text popped in first, and then everything else popped in after, the main picture of the story last.

The main picture was of the murder victim, smiling, posing with his wife at a party of some sort.

Tom recognized him, recognized him clear as day. He didn't recognize the smile, but he knew the man. Even the woman, his wife, also smiling in the picture.

He remembered him, from just days prior, from when he had tried to rip off Gutsy's head, and then was pulled from the arena.

Sam was his name.

Tom felt a tear rise in the corner of his eye and he wiped it away hastily, and his eyes tore through the article, searching it desperately for information.

Samuel Harrington was the man's full name. He'd been out downtown, near the arena, drinking at a bar, before leaving. His BAC was a .22, very drunk. He'd been bludgeoned to death, and his body ripped apart.

And some of it was missing.

Tom's eyes scanned the rest of the article, but he wasn't taking in any more information, and then he thought, he thought a terrible thought, and looked to the date of the man's death.

He'd been killed the night of Tuesday the 17th.

The same night he'd been thrown out of the arena for assaulting Gutsy.

The same night as Tom's first nightmare.

9

Tom got up from the computer, pacing.

It had to be a coincidence. A terrible, terrible coincidence.

He could make it make sense in his mind. A dude like Sam was disagreeable, aggressive. Hell, he started a fight with Gutsy just because the clown threw his hat. He was mean to his wife. He could have picked a fight with the wrong person, and the wrong person killed him.

Yeah, that had to be it. It just happened to align with the same night he fought with Tom. That had to be it.

Yeah, that makes sense in a vacuum. But don't be a fucking idiot, Tom. You remember the nightmare. And this isn't an isolated incident. Sam was one of many.

Tom remembered his mother's words. *They're starting up*

again.

What was starting up again? More murders. Tom hadn't heard of any murders, but then again, he didn't pay attention to the news. He was too busy drowning in debt. If the problem wasn't right outside his front door, he couldn't pay attention to it. Skates had mentioned deaths too, hadn't he?

He took a breath and went back to the computer, and dug further in, opening up new tabs with links to other reports, all of them connected to Sam's murder.

His mother hadn't been wrong. There had been a series of murders like this, dating back several months. They'd come in fits and starts—two here, one here, three here—and then subside for a week or two. None of the victims were connected to each other, and all were brutally killed, with the bodies mutilated after death, with pieces missing. And all of the deaths happened downtown, specifically all within a few blocks of the arena. The killing last night was the farthest from the arena, almost a mile away.

Sam's death wasn't an isolated incident. He wasn't killed because he picked a fight with some serious hombre. He'd been killed by the same serial killer.

The same night as your first nightmare.

It didn't mean anything. How could it? He'd had plenty of nightmares throughout his life. Almost all of them were driven by stress, and all involved being late for something, or losing his driver's license, or forgetting to do something important. Hell, in the last couple months, he'd had more nightmares than he'd had in his whole life, inspired by debt and anxiety about having a place to stay in a month or two.

But they weren't nightmares about hunting someone. About feeding on someone, Tom. And they were never, ever bathed in visions of red.

Tom paced again. His mind raced, trying to think of something, anything, that could explain what he'd seen. He had the knowledge, inside of him, that the first nightmare came when he wore the Gutsy suit. It was there, lurking, but he'd put it aside. He had dismissed it as anxiety from being attacked. Of course, of course, when you wore the Gutsy suit, you saw the world through red. The trauma of being attacked, the subconscious experience of seeing red—it had led to the nightmare.

That's what he told himself, quickly, and then moved on.

But then it'd happened again, and now with the knowledge of the murders, multiple murders—his mind couldn't keep up.

But it was only the two deaths, Sam, and last night. What about the eight others?

He hadn't had nightmares with them. Hell, he didn't even know about them until right now.

Simple, buddy. You had only started wearing the suit for the last two.

But what did that mean? Tom didn't know. He sat down again, and shut his laptop closed, pulling out a notebook, and flipping to an empty page. Tom grabbed a pencil, and scrawled notes, connecting them with lines, outlining all the info he had. He could rationalize this. He could make it make sense.

A series of murders, including the man who had attacked him. Wearing the Gutsy suit. Nightmare visions in Red.

He finished and looked at the paper. Those people were dead, that was for sure. Everything else—he didn't know.

Had he seen them being hunted?

And hunted by what?

His mind flashed to an answer, the only answer in reach, but he couldn't broach that, not yet, because that way laid madness. He couldn't follow that path, not without more evidence.

But what evidence could he gather? The police wouldn't tell him anything. They would arrest him, maybe, but they sure as hell wouldn't tell him any more details about the murders.

He thought, still pacing. Who else had experience in the suit?

Shannon.

But could he ask her? She'd been in the suit more than anyone, but had looked at him cross-eyed when he'd asked about nightmares. If he started asking about killings, she'd go straight to Barbara, and he'd be out of a job.

Maybe that wouldn't be the worst thing.

He pushed the thought away. He had to know. His stomach ached, just at the thought of those deaths, of even being close to them. Even Sam, the bully, didn't deserve a death like that.

Maybe he would go to Shannon if he had more evidence, but he'd have to collect that first. But how?

Then he remembered. Skates and Shannon had both said they'd gone through a lot of employees lately. People who'd come in, and then after a couple days, ghosted them. No two weeks notice, nothing. They just vanished.

Could they have seen the same things Tom had?

Maybe. It made sense. If he could talk to them. Even just one of them.

But how would he get in touch with them? HR wouldn't

give them contact info for old employees. He couldn't ask Shannon. Unless—

*

"What the hell are you doing here today, kid?" asked Skates. He sat in his little office, his white hair glowing underneath the fluorescent lights.

"I wanted to talk to you," said Tom. He thought about calling Skates, but seeing him in person was a better bet, anyway. Plus, the drive gave him a chance to think of a story to tell Skates, so he'd cough up the contact info, provided he had it.

"About what?" asked Skates. "Everything alright? I saw there was another killing last night. So awful, some young girl, head of her class—just awful."

"Everything is fine," said Tom, lying through his teeth. "I was just wondering if you had any contact info about any of the guys who played Gutsy before me. Phone numbers, emails, anything."

"I mean, I'd have to check," said Skates. "Maybe—wait, why do you want to talk to those guys? You got the job, and Shannon says you're lights out—I don't think you need advice."

"Oh no," said Tom. "It's not for advice." He looked thoughtful. "Shannon said that one of them took a notebook of hers, which had a bunch of ideas for skits in it. You know, stuff she wanted to try with Gutsy, during games. She said there was a lot in there, but one of the guys took it. I suggested we hunt them down, get it back, but she dismissed it, out of hand. Said it wasn't worth the trouble."

"You want to get it back?" asked Skates.

"Yeah," said Tom. "Shannon has already done so much for me. I want to at least try."

"You're a good kid, Tommy," said Skates. "Let me look." Skates pulled out his phone and pawed at it with his big hands. "Do you remember which one it was? We've gone through a couple—"

"I'm not sure if I remember the name. Who do you have?"

"I think I only got numbers for the last guy," said Skates.

"What's his name?"

"Steven Page," said Skates.

"Oh, that's it!" said Tom. "She said it was Steve who took it."

"Well, I've got a couple numbers for him," said Skates. "Don't know which is which, honestly. Guy was flighty, hard to get a hold of. Didn't surprise me when he left without a word."

"Can I have them?" asked Tom.

"Sure," said Skates. Skates scribbled the two numbers down on a post-it note. He handed it over. "I didn't give you this, alright? I'm pretty sure HR don't want me handing over personal info like this."

"Mum's the word," said Tom. "Thanks, Skates."

"Good luck, kid," said Skates. "I won't tell Shannon."

"I appreciate it," said Tom.

*

The phone rang and rang, and then went to voicemail.

"Hey, this is Steve. Leave a message and I'll get back to

you," said a male voice, and Tom hung up without leaving a message.

He tried the other number.

An answer after three rings. "Hello?" answered a woman's voice.

"Uh, hi. I'm calling for a Steven Page," said Tom. "Is he available?"

"No," said the voice. "I told you to stop calling. I gave the police all the information I had. Please leave me alone. Just because he put me as a second on the account doesn't mean I'm accountable for his debt. I've talked to a lawyer about it, and I will—"

"No, please," said Tom. "I don't know what you're talking about. I'm an investigator hired by the Baltimore Brawlers. We lost touch with Steven after he was hired by the team, and they wanted me to find him."

Silence on the other end.

"Ma'am, you there?" asked Tom.

"Steve is dead," said the woman. "I don't want to talk about it anymore. Please, don't call me—"

Tom's stomach sank. *Oh God.*

"Please, ma'am," said Tom. "Please don't hang up. I'm very sorry to hear that. The team was not aware, but they would absolutely want to know the details, and help in any way they can."

"Really?" she asked. "He only worked for them for a couple weeks—"

"When you join the team, you're family," said Tom. "What's your name?"

"Andrea," she said. "I've had debt collectors hounding me for weeks, just because my name was listed as contact info on some credit card account he had. I don't have the money to pay them, we weren't married. Steve is dead. I—"

"If you fill me in on the details, I can have the team take care of it for you," said Tom. "Do you have time to meet today to chat? Over coffee?"

"You promise they'll take care of these damn phone calls?" asked Andrea.

"Absolutely," said Tom, with as much sincerity as he could muster.

"Then yes," said Andrea. "I don't work until five. We can meet this morning. There's a cafe on the corner."

Within an hour, Tom sat across from Andrea at the small cafe. Andrea was short, her black hair cut into a pixie. Her sweater engulfed her. She drank a latte.

"So, what do you want to know?" she asked.

"Just the broad details about his departure from the job," said Tom. "He just disappeared without warning. The team was a little surprised."

"Do you work for the team?" asked Andrea.

"I work with them, if that makes sense," said Tom. "Not exclusively."

"Well, that job was the beginning of the end for him."

"What do you mean?"

"I don't know," said Andrea. "Sometimes I think if Steve hadn't gotten the job playing Gutsy, he'd still be alive. Maybe I'm wrong. Maybe it was just a matter of time, and it was a coincidence that it was Gutsy that started the spiral."

"Spiral?"

"Yeah," she said. "I don't know how else to describe it. He was desperate for work. I couldn't pay the rent by myself. He'd been laid off at his last job. He saw the job listing for

Gutsy and kind of just took a shot in the dark. He'd worked in theater in college, he liked hockey and thought, why not? It paid well enough. Turns out he was what they needed." She took a sip of her latte. "But it killed him."

"It killed him?" asked Tom. His mind was racing. He tried to keep himself calm.

"Not literally," said Andrea. "But once he stepped into that suit, he changed. It sounds ridiculous at face value, but that's what happened. Literally, the first time he wore the Gutsy suit, he came back a different person. It was small things at first. He was more irritable. He couldn't sleep well, kept tossing and turning, and I'm a light sleeper, so it meant I didn't sleep well either. After a few times in the suit, he was just downright angry, when we were together."

"Was he an angry guy?"

"No, not at all," said Andrea. "He was laid back. One of the things I liked about him. I've had my share of aggro dudes, and I'm done with them. It had me questioning our relationship." She wiped away a tear. "I had thought, up until that point, that maybe he was the dude I'd marry."

"I'm—I'm sorry," said Tom.

"Not your fault," said Andrea. "But he would be angry, for no reason." She took a deep breath. "And then he started having nightmares."

"Nightmares? About what?" asked Tom, already knowing the answer.

"Red," said Andrea. "Nightmares about being in red. That's all he would ever say. I would try and pick more from him, but he was never clear. He would just repeat that, over and over again. And I could tell when he had them, because he'd be even worse. But that wasn't even the worst thing?"

"What was the worst thing?"

"I mean, I get it. If you can't sleep, you're having night-mares, it can put you in a bad mood. And I really don't know what was going on at his work, but it obviously was stressing him out, but I didn't see it. I tried to be supportive—but—but all things have a limit." She took a sip of her drink, and then looked at Tom. "He started talking about Gutsy—as if—" She took a deep breath. "As if he was real."

"What?"

"He talked about him like he was just another person walking around," said Andrea. "Like if you were talking about your buddy, who lives down the street. He would tell me that Gutsy wouldn't like that, or man, I hope Gutsy is in a good mood today."

"I—" started Tom, but he didn't know what to say. His guts ached.

"I didn't know what to do," said Andrea. "What could I do? I tried to get him help, I did. I wanted him to talk to someone, but even seeing a therapist was way out of our budget. And even then—I didn't realize it was so bad. It happened so fast. Within a few days of that, he wasn't just talking about Gutsy. He was *afraid* of him. Afraid of him, afraid of playing him. I couldn't make heads or tails of it. I seriously thought about getting him committed. He was ranting and raving by the end, and before I could do any-thing, he left. Ran out of the house."

"How—how did he die?"

"He killed himself," said Andrea. "Jumped off a bridge. They found his body in the water."

"Oh, god, I'm so sorry," said Tom.

"Thank you," said Andrea. "Does that answer your questions?"

"Well, sort of," said Tom, wincing. "I think it honestly gives me more questions to answer."

"It's good to know I'm not the only one with them," said Andrea. "I've been left in the lurch. I had to move out, uproot everything." She sighed again, staring at her coffee. "Do you want me to write down my information?"

"Yeah," said Tom. "That'd be great. I'll hand this over to our HR and legal teams. They should be able to help you."

"I appreciate it," said Andrea. "You know, I thought it was hilarious at first. My boyfriend would play that dumb muppet. But now—now, I hate that damn thing. I want it to burn, forever."

10

What the hell did it all mean?

Steven had worn the suit, and he had killed himself. He had the nightmares, the same as Tom. He'd fallen apart, started thinking Gutsy was real, and had committed suicide.

Had Steve seen the deaths as well? Is that what drove him to kill himself?

But Andrea was right. The nightmares were the tip of the iceberg. Steve had thought Gutsy was alive.

Tom stared at his notebook, back at his apartment. He had written down everything Andrea had said, adding it to his piles of notes, trying to piece it all together.

Steve had the nightmares, just like he did. Seeing into a red world. Had he seen the same thing Tom did? Had he seen people being hunted?

Tom wasn't alone, at least in the nightmares. And the only thing that Steve and him shared was they both wore the Gutsy costume. They both had slid it on, and done the song and dance for the crowd at Brawlers games.

There was something wrong with the suit, had to be. Couldn't be a coincidence, not on that scale.

But why didn't the same thing happen to Shannon?

Tom didn't know. Either she was lying, or it was something else, like it only affected men. But he doubted that.

She was hiding something.

But why did Steve think Gutsy was real? Why did he talk about him as if he was alive?

And who was killing people?

Tom looked at the paper, the memories of his nightmares echoing in his head. Visions of the Red, and of murder, and of a predator.

The answer stared at him, right in the face, but he couldn't believe it. It was impossible, and the mere thought of it put him in the same category as Steve, a man who had become disconnected from reality.

Steve thought Gutsy was alive, because *he was alive.*

Alive, and hunting people, at night.

But why, and how? And why did Tom see those nightmares? Why did he see what Gutsy saw?

Tom stood up, and ran his hands over his face, squeezing his eyes shut.

And what the hell would he do with this information? He couldn't go to the cops and tell them a damn hockey mascot was killing people. They'd send him right to the psych ward. He could tell Shannon, or Skates.

But would they believe him?

Or did Shannon already know?

Or—was it Shannon in the suit?

Was she killing people dressed as Gutsy?

But how did that explain the nightmares?

Tom collapsed into his bed, face down.

He couldn't do this. He should just quit this job and leave it all behind him.

Cloudy gave you that cash. He called you family.

That was all well and good, but Cloudy was a millionaire hockey player. Tom's normal salary was not enough to put up with killer hockey mascots. He had paid off his back rent, fixed his car, and he could find another job to pay the bills.

It's not about that, not anymore, and you know it. Those people died, Tom. Died brutally. If you run, it'll keep happening.

They weren't his responsibility. They weren't, they weren't.

He pushed himself out of his bed, and went into the bathroom, and turned on the shower.

He would take a shower, and take his mind off of everything, and let the answer come to him.

The hot water pelted him, and he stood there, letting it cascade over him. With just the water hitting him, with no other senses, he could focus. He could meditate here, and let all the thoughts out of him.

He wanted to run, wanted to flee this job, just like the others had. Tom knew now they had left because they had all experienced the same thing he had. They had seen the world in red, had watched someone be hunted, and had ducked out. It wasn't worth what money they were paid.

He wanted to run, but he couldn't. It had nothing to do

with the job, or with Cloudy calling him family. It had to do with letting people die without stepping in. He had to try something.

But what?

What could he do?

He needed proof, some sort of evidence, even if it was just seeing it, with his own two eyes. Not vague memories of nightmares. Not what somebody heard someone else say. He needed to see it.

And he had to rule out Shannon's involvement.

How could he do it?

He would have to catch Gutsy in the act. He'd have to see it, with his own two eyes. It would be enough proof. Not only for others, but for himself. Because no matter how much it made sense, he couldn't believe it. It was impossible.

But a part of him hoped Gutsy was alive, some strange entity. Because the other explanation was even worse. That Shannon was using the suit to commit grisly murders.

Well, he knew what he needed to do. But how would he do it? How could he catch Gutsy in the act?

He thought, letting the hot water wash over him, and the idea hit him. Would it work? He didn't know.

But he had to try.

He shut off the water.

*

Tom stared at Gutsy's head. It sat on the break room table, its angry eyes staring dead at him, filled with nothing.

The last two killings had only happened after he had worn the suit. If he truly wanted to test his hypothesis, he would have to put the costume on, and see if it was connected.

It was late, and the arena was empty. He was sure there was security, sitting at a desk somewhere, monitoring some camera feeds, but he was an employee and had access to everything. If they cared, they could stop him, but why would they? If they questioned him, he could just say he was rehearsing with the suit. He really only didn't want to run into Skates or Shannon, and neither would be here this late on a non-game day.

He wasn't worried about security.

His main worry was putting on the head. He had the rest of the suit on, but he stared into the eyes of Gutsy.

"Have I gone crazy?" he asked the face of Gutsy. "Are you alive? Was Steve right? Are they going to be asking the same questions about me, that I asked about Steve?"

Gutsy stared back at him. Tom looked, waiting, but no answer came. Tom was half-glad he didn't get one, because he didn't know what he'd do if the suit answered him.

But he had to work up the guts to put it on.

He stood up from his seat, breaking his gaze with Gutsy, and paced, back and forth, clenching his fists, taking deep breaths, and then he turned, and moving quickly, grabbed the head and plopped it on top of him, sliding it down until the headrest inside slid softly into place. Every time was easier. He knew the suit now.

Or the suit knew *him*.

The world was red, again, but not the red from his nightmare. Merely a soft red coating over the world he knew, a cheap facsimile of his perspective in his nightmares.

But now what?

Tom didn't know. He left the break room and walked through the concourse, doing laps around the entire arena. He walked slowly, feeling the suit move with him, feeling the floor through Gutsy's feet. Tom looked around, trying to feel Gutsy's perspective. Remembering how he felt when he held the t-shirt cannon in his arms. That sudden rage. The need to inflict violence without cause and justification. The thirst, the blood lust.

But he couldn't summon it. It wasn't the same, not without being surrounded by crowds, by people, by targets.

He did lap after lap, waiting for something, but there was nothing. Tom suddenly felt like everything that had transpired the past couple days was all in his head, all a series of coincidences that had simply overwhelmed him. He returned to the locker room, so he could change out of the suit.

Oh, fuck.

He had never taken the head off by himself. Even when he closed up alone, there was always someone there to help him get Gutsy's head off.

He could do it.

He reached up, and squeezed right where he could feel it, to break the hold the headrest had on him, and then pulled up, as hard as he could.

It always got stuck on the way off, and that held true again today, as it stuck to his head, and no matter how hard he tugged, it stayed put.

Goddamnit, goddamnit, please, get this fucking thing off me—

He yanked, and a burst of anger rose in his heart, just for a second, and then the head slid off, the internal headrest coming loose, and it was in his hands, and he dropped it on the table, hating the idea of holding it anymore.

He turned from it, still wearing the rest of the suit. Tom felt stupid. This was dumb, and empty. None of this made any sense.

Pffphww

Tom turned back toward the sound. He looked at Gutsy, his head sitting on the break table, its empty eyes staring directly at Tom. There was no one else here. Tom glanced around. Then the air kicked on again, keeping the cold arena warm.

Must have been the vents.

He should put the suit away. If this was going to work, he had to put the costume away. He took off the torso, arms and legs, and then stashed them along with the head in the normal spot, safely in the small closet they kept it in.

Gutsy's eyes watched as he closed the door on him.

"Jesus Christ, Tom," he said. "If you weren't crazy before, you're definitely crazy now."

Still, he had come this far. He would play this until the end. Tom left the arena, the same way he came in, and retreated to his car. He had parked at the edge of the employee parking area, right on the verge between the arena and downtown. The arena wasn't technically downtown, but only a thin strip of railroad separated the two, and after and before each game, thousands would pour back and forth between them, funneling a bunch of business into downtown bars and restaurants.

Tom got into his car, with a newly repaired brake line, and sat in the driver's seat. He was cold, but he wouldn't turn on the heat until absolutely necessary. His jacket kept him warm enough, at least for now.

If Gutsy wanted to get to downtown, he'd have to move past Tom. Of all the permutations of his idea, this felt like the most solid. He thought to wander downtown, but it was a massive area, and there was no way he could cover the entire space. He could sit right outside the arena, but there were a hundred entrances and exits. This was the choke point. This felt right.

But did Gutsy move like people at all? In his nightmares, he seemed to flow like water, and supernaturally avoid being seen. But those were dreams, and hazy ones at that. Tom had no idea if anything inside them was real or not. He would trust Gutsy followed normal physics until proven otherwise.

He waited. People wandered by, without a second glance into the shadows of his car.

An hour passed, and then another, and there was no sign of the red mascot. Tom thought to look at his phone to pass the time, but it would give him away. He would have to be vigilant. He would have to stay awake, without his phone. Even if he had been woken up before dawn by his mother, he could do it, keep his eyes open—

CRASH

Tom opened his eyes to the sound of a bottle breaking. A pair of men walked by a few dozen feet away. One had tossed a bottle into the street where it had broken.

He'd fallen asleep. Tom looked at the clock. It'd only been fifteen minutes. He hoped he hadn't missed Gutsy, lumbering into downtown to prey again. The two men wandered off, talking loudly to each other.

This was stupid. He was sitting in his car, waiting for a

damn mascot to just walk out of the arena to downtown.

"Go home, Tom," he said. "You're freezing cold. You're tired. Go home. Just quit your damn job. Go find a normal one. You're out of the hole now. You have some time."

He took a breath, and reached for his keys, and then he saw a glimpse of red in his peripheral vision.

He froze.

What was that?

He moved his eyes only, keeping his body still, looking toward where he saw the glimpse of red.

Something in the shadows shifted again, flickers of red shining into his vision, as brief points of light bounced off it.

It moved through the shadows in the night, and still, a part of Tom wanted to deny that it was him. That it was Gutsy.

But then he saw the eyes, and they were unmistakable, and Gutsy emerged into the light, lumbering, looming, seven feet tall, walking into downtown, emerging from the shadow.

Tom stayed frozen in the darkness of his car, staring at Gutsy as he walked. The shadows clung to the creature, and it lumbered at a slow but steady pace, the red fur, the huge mane swinging below its massive head.

It was absurd, ridiculous, this thing moving on its own. It was impossible, but it existed, and the part of his mind that disbelieved he pushed away. He *saw* it.

It moved, assuredly, and then Tom glimpsed movement out of the corner of his eye, and he saw a couple walking, a man and a woman, and he glanced back and Gutsy had moved, disappeared. The couple was oblivious, hadn't seen Gutsy, and continued walking, probably heading to their car.

Within a minute they were out of sight, and then Tom looked, scanning everything for Gutsy, and then suddenly, he was there again, emerging from nowhere, the shadows obeying him. Gutsy moved, and then he was on the edge of Tom's vision, past him, moving into the downtown, and Tom had to move. His plan hadn't extended past this, largely because he had been so unsure it would need to.

But he moved, he had to follow, and he left his car, into the chill night air, his breath coming out in clouds.

There was no steam coming off Gutsy at all.

Tom closed the door as quietly as he could and followed, Gutsy still a hundred feet ahead of him, moving with purpose. It reminded him of the walk of Michael Myers, never slowing, never speeding, only one constant, methodical pace.

The edges of downtown were empty, but as they moved into the more central part, there were quite a few people on the street. But Gutsy didn't stop.

He shifted.

Tom had only seen it from inside his own vision, but he saw it now in the open. Gutsy walked down the sidewalk, and every few moments, he would *shift*, disappearing, and reappearing in another place. Always within view, but never close. Fifteen or twenty feet away, in a corner, in a shadow, and then he would continue. No one reacted, no one saw him.

Except for Tom. Tom watched, and followed, staying at a distance.

Gutsy moved, still at the same pace, and now, in the heart of downtown, he turned down an alley. Tom was still a hundred feet away, and he hurried, crossing a street against the light, only glancing for a second, hoping he wouldn't be hit by a car, but he couldn't lose him, he had to keep up with Gutsy.

A few seconds of hurrying later, Tom followed after him, and he saw him, halfway down the long alley, past a dumpster.

And then Tom realized they weren't alone in the alley. There was someone else, past Gutsy, another figure in the shadows. Gutsy wasn't moving either, only standing there, watching.

Tom moved, as quiet as he could, careful of every footstep, taking quiet breaths. He crept up, slowing still, and hid behind one of the few dumpsters that broke up the space. He peeked his head around the corner of the dumpster, and Gutsy was right there, his back to Tom, staring at the man in front of him, who was unaware. Tom listened, and he realized the man was taking a piss, his back to Gutsy.

Fuck fuck fuck.

He should say something, Gutsy was going to kill him, and all of this in the abstract abruptly became very, very real, and Tom knew he should shout out, he should warn the man, but he suddenly realized his own vulnerability, his own danger, and if he said a word, he would be Gutsy's next target, and all of this happened in a moment and then the man turned and Gutsy stood there, and before the man uttered a sound Gutsy swiped his large clawed red hand in an instant and ripped out the man's throat.

Blood spurted from the man's neck as he desperately tried to hold it in, tried to scream, but nothing came, only gore and blood, and then he fell, and then Gutsy bent over his struggling body and plunged his hands into his torso, ripping his guts out, strings of organs and intestines flying to the side.

Tom looked away then, his eyes closed, his breath held. Gutsy couldn't know he was there, he'd be next. He had to get away, had to run.

And then Gutsy fed.

11

Gutsy's red hands had turned into meat hooks, ripping out the victim's guts with barbaric strength, the sound of flesh splitting and organs tearing filling the alley. Tom heard the sounds, and smelled the copper scent of blood as it filled the space.

Oh God oh God

It was impossible, this was impossible, that's what he had said, this was just a test, just a test, something to see if Gutsy was a real, an unthinkable hypothesis that turned out true and now this man was dead, sparked by him wearing the Gutsy suit again, and now he knew why Steven Page had killed himself, it's because he had awoken Gutsy, had em-powered it to kill and to eat. Tom looked again, he had to look, this was his burden to bear.

He turned, and he watched Gutsy pull out lengths of intestines, his red fur even darker now, stained dark with gallons of blood, and he opened his terrible maw, and inside it wasn't foam and fake fur, but an endless void that slurped the six foot long pieces of intestines down like wet noodles, and Tom gagged and almost threw up, forcing himself quiet.

Gutsy fed greedily, shoveling meat into his mouth, but it wasn't just the blood, or the meat, or *guts* he fed upon, but something else as well. Tom didn't know what it was, but it was palpable. There was a feeling in the air, of transmission, and he watched Gutsy closely, and he stood in the cold, steam rising from the warmth of the body, from the blood, and he saw it, he swear he saw it, saw it the same way he saw it in his nightmares, saw it the way Gutsy saw it. The Red. The force of pain and chaos sown upon the world by Gutsy's violence. By the force of death.

Tom thought to run, to sprint away now, he had to, he had to get away before Gutsy saw him.

But he couldn't. He was frozen out of fear, fear of being seen by this terrible beast. If he ran, if Gutsy saw him, would he be next? Would he be ripped apart, his guts thrown into the dark void that was Gutsy's innards? Would he feed that insatiable hunger, help to fill that dreadful well, not only with his blood, but with the chaos, with the pain caused by his death, by the tears his mother cried when she learned her only child was the next victim of the serial killer that she so desperately feared?

So he froze, and tucked himself as tight as he could, and found a small crevice behind the dumpster he hid next to, and forced himself in, quiet, the wet sound of blood still splashing as Gutsy drove himself deep into the corpse, his hands now serving as spades, finding the valuable meat he so craved.

Tom winced as the sounds continued, for an eternity, his eyes closed, his breath shallow—

Please, please go, please go back, Gutsy, go back to your storage closet—

He couldn't take it much longer. He would scream, scream with his entire lungs and then Gutsy would dig those sudden spade hands into his stomach and spill every-thing inside him onto the ground where he would steam into the air.

But then the wet sounds stopped.

They were no more, and Tom split his eyes open, and the figure of Gutsy walked back past him, out onto the street, disappearing and appearing, gliding along the nooks and crannies of the shadows as he avoided eyesight, and then he was gone.

Tom waited, waited, and he *was* gone, and he took a deep breath, even if the breath was filled with copper and blood.

Tears pushed their way to the edge of his eyes, but he forced them down. Tom couldn't cry, not now. He pulled himself out of the crevice he'd tucked himself into, and looked after Gutsy, to the street. He should leave, leave now.

But he turned, turned to see the carnage. It was his bur-den, and he must look, and see the horrible aftermath.

And it was horrible. It—it didn't look like a body at all. His eyes flitted over what was left of the poor man, and al-most all of it was destroyed, ripped into pieces. It looked like the man had been thrown into a meat grinder, only his head recognizable as a formerly human trait. Tom swallowed back bile and turned away. He couldn't look, not anymore.

He should call the police. Tell them someone had been killed, and they needed to come—

Are they going to arrest Gutsy? No, of course not. They'll come, and they'll arrest you.

He wanted to do something, something to help with the terrible creature he had unleashed. But nothing could be done, not now. This man was dead, torn to pieces, his guts food for the endless well of hunger that was Gutsy.

"What the hell are you doing?" asked a voice, from the other end of the alley, and Tom glanced back to see the silhouette, and panic filled him, and he ran, ran the same way Gutsy did, sprinted as hard as he ever had. He pulled up his hood as he raced, breath coming hard and hot in the cold, cold air. If they found him there, at the sight of the murder, they would blame him, even if it was impossible for him to have done it, not without a wood chipper—

But it was your fault, you unleashed that thing—

He sprinted to his car, not looking back, and the crowds thinned, and soon he was back in his car, and he started it up, and the tires squealed as he drove onto the interstate, and away.

He tried to catch his breath, and his defrost desperately tried to defog the windshield, and his heart beat hard, hard in his chest, and then the tears came, pouring out of him.

He sobbed, sobbed hopelessly, pulling off dangerously to the shoulder on the interstate, cars rocketing past him, his car shaking with the wind.

He cried and cried, the horrible sounds and smells and sights filling his mind, and he wept until there were no more tears. He reached into the dirty glove box, pulling out fast food napkins to wipe his face and blow his nose, throwing them to the side.

Tom did his best to breathe. He took deep breaths, and slowed down his heart rate. When he could breathe again, he looked into his mirror and pulled his car back onto the interstate, accelerating as well as the beaten car could.

He was home within ten minutes, riding in silence, his mind empty, blissfully empty, after the onslaught of terrible sensation that night.

He got home, and went inside his apartment. He sat on the bed and stared into nothing.

What could he do?

What should he do?

He remembered suddenly, the belief earlier that maybe it was Shannon in the suit, perpetrating these horrendous crimes.

But Shannon didn't do that, not unless she had suddenly gained an incredible strength and the ability to flow like water through the shadows and along the nooks and crannies of buildings.

No, she hadn't done any of it.

But she had worn the suit. And she had lied about her nightmares. She knew more than she let on.

He opened his phone, scrolled to her name, and called.

It rang a dozen times, and he was waiting for it to go to voicemail, but then she answered.

"H—hello?" she answered, her voice bleary. If there was still any question that she was in the suit, that answered it. No one would have committed that murder, that terrible mutilation, and then been able to answer the phone not thirty minutes later like that.

"Shannon, it's Tom," he said.

"Tom?" she asked. "What the fuck? What time is it?"

"It's almost two in the morning," he said, his voice quiet.

"What the hell are you calling me for?" she asked, her voice a little more awake.

"I saw him, Shannon."

A pause.

"Saw who?"

"Gutsy, Shannon," said Tom. "I saw him. I followed him. He killed someone. Tonight."

"Tom—I can't—"

"No," said Tom. "We need to talk. Tonight. Now."

A long pause. Tom waited.

"I'll be over in a few. What's your address?"

12

Shannon was there in twenty minutes, bleary-eyed, wearing a big hoodie and sweats, both at least two sizes too big.

She looked bleary, but also something else.

It was guilt.

"You're drinking coffee at 2 AM?" asked Shannon.

"Oh, I don't plan on sleeping," said Tom. "Maybe tomorrow. Do you want some?"

"No, that's okay," said Shannon. Tom sat down on his couch, and Shannon sat in the small, plush chair, one Tom had gotten at a thrift store for twenty bucks.

"You wanted to talk, right?" asked Shannon. "What do you want to talk about?"

Tom paused. He took a breath. "How much do you know?"

Shannon took her own. "I—I don't know."

"Shannon—you can't keep doing this—"

"You want to know what I *know*?" asked Shannon. "I don't *know* anything. I think some things, and I suspect others, but I don't know much of anything. About all of this—I am confident in almost none of it. And I've never spoken to anyone about it. How could I?"

"You could have given me fair warning."

"Oh, really, I could have?" asked Shannon. "What did you want me to tell you? That the damn mascot for our hockey team is somehow alive, and eats people when he feels like it?"

"You could have said something when I asked about the nightmares," said Tom.

"Use sleeping pills," said Shannon. "Ambien works. Haven't had a nightmare since I've started taking them."

"You have to fucking drug yourself to sleep?"

"Do you enjoy watching that fucking thing hunt? Seeing what he sees?"

"Of course not," said Tom. "It's awful."

"Exactly," said Shannon. "So sleeping pills it was."

"That sounds miserable," said Tom.

"I get by," said Shannon.

"He's killing people, Shannon!" said Tom. "I watched it happen, it—it was horrible."

"I'm well aware," said Shannon. "Believe me, I'm aware."

Tom took a long swallow of coffee. He was on edge.

"Start from the start," said Tom. "I understand we're dealing with the unknown."

"You can fucking say that again," said Shannon. "Okay, okay. I was working for the team as an Ice Girl."

"You were an Ice Girl?" asked Tom. The Ice Girls were glorified cheerleaders, who wore skin tight outfits and did dance routines during intermission. Gutsy sometimes did skits with them. "I thought you said you were Barbara's assistant."

"I lied," said Shannon. "I have dance experience, and I needed work. But I didn't love it, and when I heard the Brawlers were working on getting a mascot, I made sure that my name was in the hat to join the mascot team." She paused. "I wish I could go back and be an Ice Girl, at this point."

"Why can't you?"

"Because it's safer with me being Gutsy," said Shannon.

"Safer?"

Shannon put her hands up for him to wait. "I made it clear to Barbara that I would love to be Gutsy. I know they had hired a designer to make the costume, and they were still going back and forth on it, and a lot of time passed with no movement whatsoever. And then one day, Gutsy just showed up."

"What do you mean, showed up?"

"The costume was there," said Shannon. "I asked around. I couldn't get a straight answer from anyone. Barbara, Skates, whoever. From what I've heard, they went back and forth on design ideas, and then the costume appeared one day. Barbara approved, and so we started using it. I was the first person on the Gutsy team, if you will. I was the first person to wear it."

"No one thought it was weird it just showed up?"

"Of course we did," said Shannon. "But also, it's just a mascot costume. Everyone assumed the designer was tired of getting notes from Barbara, and just went through with his most recent design. He'd already been paid."

"Is that what happened?"

"I don't know," said Shannon. "I didn't think about it too much, not then. I just wore the suit, and cobbled together a team. Maybe I would have looked into it on my own, but then Gutsy blew up on social media, and everything was a whirlwind. We started using him way more."

"So you truly don't know where he came from?"

"No."

"Did you get nightmares, wearing the costume?"

"Not at first," said Shannon. "At least not in the way they would become. There were no red visions. No hunting. It was more curious. Exploring. It didn't feel so ominous. I dismissed it. They were just weird dreams, and I've had plenty of weird dreams in my life."

"There was nothing else?" asked Tom. "Nothing weird while in the suit?"

"No," said Shannon. "At least not that I can place. He might have been manipulating my emotions then, but nothing I noticed. I was busy getting everything off the ground. Trying to train new people to be in the suit. I didn't want to be in it every night. Even without all the weirdness, it's hard work. It's exhausting. It's nice for someone to spell you, once in a while. And then—the first murder happened."

"Did you see it?" asked Tom. "While you slept."

"Yes," said Shannon. "It wasn't clear, you know. You're seeing everything in shades of red, but that need, that hunger, that was there. And there had been hints, maybe if I paid attention. But I had never felt it so strongly. And I knew in that nightmare, it was hunting someone."

"When did you make the connection?"

"After a couple of weeks," said Shannon. "It kept happening, and it doesn't take a brain genius to recognize the patterns."

"What did you do?"

"Nothing, at first," said Shannon. "Except go crazy. I nearly lost it. It doesn't make any sense. Gutsy is absolutely alive, somehow, but trying to tell that to anyone who hasn't worn the suit? Impossible. But everything points to it. I had never actually followed him."

"I had to know," said Tom.

"How did he not know you were watching?"

"I don't know," said Tom. "He still dodged other people's view, but not mine."

"So either it doesn't work on us because we've worn the costume—"

"Or he knew I was watching," said Tom. "Yeah. I don't like that at all."

"But how have you kept this up? I don't know how I could wear that suit again."

"Pills," said Shannon. "Sleeping pills at night. Mood stabilizers during the day. He feeds off strong emotions, especially anger and fear. If you keep them down, you can wear the costume, and he won't go out at night. At least, mostly. Until you got hired, there hadn't been any deaths in a while. I thought it was over."

"Tonight was my fault," said Tom, looking down. "I needed to know, so I went to the arena, and I put on the suit. It must have been enough to give him some juice."

Shannon sighed. "As far as I can tell, if you keep a level head and stay calm with it on, he's much less likely to wake at night. Also, much less likely to influence your emotions. The pills help, though."

"I don't want to take pills to do my job."

"I don't take pills to play Gutsy," said Shannon, her face tired. "I take pills to keep Gutsy from killing people, Tom. It's not a big deal. I don't feel that different. And it's kept that thing from eating people's guts out."

"You could quit," said Tom.

"They'd hire someone else who doesn't know how to keep it under control," said Shannon. "And I need a paycheck, Tom."

"There're a lot of jobs—"

"I need a paycheck *now*, Tom," said Shannon. "My mother is in nursing care. A good one. Where they hire enough people, and take good care of the resident. And those cost a lot of money. If I hopped to another job, I'd make less, and I can't afford it. I've done the math."

"Are you sure that it works?"

"Most of the time," said Shannon. "There's a part of Gutsy that you can't keep under wraps, not for long. It's too strong, whatever it is. It needs what it needs, and it goes and gets it."

"How can you be so calm?" asked Tom. "It's killing people!"

"I've done this for months, Tom," said Shannon. "I've done the math. What am I supposed to do? Call the cops? No. You've done the same thing I have. No one would believe us. We'd get arrested, at least for a while. Until Gutsy killed some more."

"We can destroy the suit," said Tom. "We can burn it. Or throw it into the ocean with some weights."

Shannon tightened her lips. "I've thought about it. Many,

many times."

"But you haven't tried?"

Shannon stared at him. "Do you think Gutsy knows what we think?"

"What? You mean, right now?"

"No," said Shannon. "When we wear the suit. When we slide his head, right on top of ours. Do you think he can read our mind?"

"I—" started Tom. "I don't know. It doesn't seem like it. It seems like it can only influence our emotions."

Shannon only stared at him. "I think it learned about Earth, from me," said Shannon, finally. "I don't think it knew anything, at first. But while it was on me, it learned. Those early dreams—Gutsy was figuring out how we work. How *humans* work. And when he figured that out, it was time to feed."

"What are you getting at?"

"What if he knows about my mom?" asked Shannon. "What if he's seen my thoughts about her? About the other people I care about? About the people *you* care about?"

Tom stared back. He thought to his worried mother, watching too much news.

"Because of course I've thought about destroying the suit. I would tell Barbara, and Skates, and all the higher ups, that it was an accident. I'm smart enough. I'd make it look convincing. They'd be upset. They'd get a replacement suit commissioned, but at least, the real Gutsy would be gone." Shannon swallowed. "I'm not worried about that. The reason I haven't tried to wipe that fucking thing off the face of the Earth is because what if I can't? What if I douse it in gasoline, and set it on fire, and it doesn't burn?"

"The victim, a few nights ago," said Tom. "It was the dude who attacked me. Attacked Gutsy. He holds grudges."

"I know," said Shannon. "He's vindictive. He's petty. The same gags that go viral on social media aren't as funny when instead of throwing your hat, he's chopping your fucking head off. So, what if I try and destroy the suit, and Gutsy doesn't like it? What if Gutsy decides that our relationship, whatever the hell you want to call it, doesn't serve him anymore, and he chooses to be petty, and vindictive, and in the middle of the night, he devours my fucking mother in the middle of her nursing home?"

Shannon's eyes shined with tears, and silence hung between them.

"So, I'm sorry that I didn't tell you. You understand better than anyone how impossible that conversation is. But now that you know, you can manage him better. We can keep him under control."

"I don't want to keep him under control, Shannon," said Tom. "I want to stop him."

"I'm not saying we can't try," said Shannon. "Now that there's two of us, maybe we can do it. But we have to very, very, careful."

Tom took a deep breath. "Okay."

"The off-site event is tomorrow," said Shannon. "Business as usual, for now."

"Who'll wear the costume?"

Shannon stared at him. "I'll wear it. I know him better."

13

"Welcome, everyone!" yelled Amy, standing at the impromptu podium. "The Brawlers would love to welcome you all to the opening of the new Becker's location, conveniently located in the heart of the Pinewood Shopping Center!"

Amy addressed the small crowd of a couple hundred people, all haphazardly gathered in the modest, cordoned off area of the parking lot. Tom stood nearby, wearing his standard Gutsy handling outfit. Shannon was next to him as Gutsy. They were on the stage, on the side, alongside Cloudy, and a bunch of other people Tom didn't know.

He didn't need to know. All he needed to do was make sure Gutsy didn't murder anyone. The fake job of handling Gutsy had become all too real.

Tom knew Shannon was inside Gutsy right now, and in control of him. But he couldn't help but feel wary being so close to the monster. All the blood and gore was gone from Gutsy when they retrieved him this morning. He was exactly where Tom had left him. Gutsy had betrayed nothing about his late night murder. Tom's heart beat hard in his chest, and his hands felt clammy, even in the chilly winter air. He had to be alert.

"Becker's is the grocery shopping partner with the Brawlers, and we couldn't be more excited to help open up the new location," said Amy. "With a few words, here is President and CEO of Becker's Grocery, Jeremy Becker!"

A late middle-aged man in a suit that Tom couldn't pick out of a lineup walked up to the podium.

"Thank you, Amy," he said. Tom had shopped at Becker's his whole life, and it was weird standing so close to the dude who owned it. Tom knew Becker's was founded a hundred years ago or something, making this guy the grandson, or maybe great-grandson, of the original founder. Whatever. He was another super rich white guy. Tom felt more empathy for Gutsy than he did for him.

"Becker's is an institution in Baltimore," said Jeremy, addressing the crowd. It sounded like a speech he'd said a hundred times. He probably had. "We consider ourselves a family business, and with this new location in Pinewood, we hope you will welcome us into your homes, and use our products on a daily basis. We strive to make our stores a part of the city, an important part of all your lives. Thank you for letting us in." The audience politely applauded, and Jeremy paused for a moment, looking out over them. "I think that's enough of me yakking. Let's get the guy out here that you wanted to see. Tanner, come on over here!"

Cloudy left his spot next to Gutsy and walked to the podium, where Jeremy gave him a big handshake, which Cloudy returned, Cloudy dwarfing the businessman. The crowd cheered hard.

Tom had studied on Tanner Cloud since Cloudy had given him that money, and Tom now knew why Cloudy was so important. He had spent his entire career with the Brawlers, and led them to their only Stanley Cup victory, over a decade ago. They had never been back, but none of the fans cared. Cloudy was one of *them*.

"Hey folks," said Cloudy. "It's nice to see you. I love doing these things, because I get to see all of you." The crowd cheered again. "I'm not much of a speaker, but I really appreciate what Jeremy said about family, and it's one reason why I'm glad we partner with Becker's. It's not a thing you think about too often, but your grocery store is so important to your life, and believe me, what Jeremy says, he believes. I want to thank you all for coming out to this little thing, and I can't wait to meet you all, say hi, and get some pictures taken. Go Brawlers!" The people clapped again, even louder this time, and then Jeremy came back, accompanied by a bunch of other suits, and along with Cloudy, they grabbed a big pair of scissors and cut through the red tape.

Tom watched Cloudy as he helped with the festivities.

He really believes it.

This was all PR and marketing nothing, Tom knew. But Cloudy didn't care. He genuinely cared about all these people, and he truly believed what he said. Cloudy practiced what he preached. Any criticism you had of him, insincerity was not one of them. Cloudy smiled for all the publicity shots, and it was an easy smile.

They brought in Gutsy for a few photos as well, and Tom only eyed the large pair of scissors, a big prop that could easily be turned around and disembowel any of them.

But Gutsy did his normal wacky antics, messing with all the suits, and they all loved it. They knew that doing things with Gutsy earned them clout, and there was nothing more valuable than that to them.

And then the ceremony was over, and all the suits left, packed into luxury cars with chauffeurs, and then it was only the PR arm of both companies there.

They moved onto the meet and greets, with photo ops, for both Gutsy, and Cloudy. The fans were eager to meet both. Tom kept his eyes peeled. This was fairly standard, Shannon had explained. They would do some PR, some people would get a picture and a signature, and they would go home happy, with good memories of the Brawlers and whatever brand they were partnered with.

Still, Tom had his eyes on Gutsy like a hawk. It was the middle of the day in the suburbs, so he had little concern about some drunk getting too rough with Gutsy. Almost all the people there were families, with a lot of children, excited to meet Cloudy and Gutsy. Most were more excited for Gutsy, with Cloudy's best playing days behind him. Cloudy was the captain, and he got the PR attention, but he hadn't led the team in points for a solid five years.

Still, everyone was happy to see them.

It was a parade of people, the line moving quickly. They would see Gutsy first, and then Cloudy, and then they would move on, and maybe even go shopping at the store, which had technically opened for the first time that morning.

Shannon was a pro at this, able to interact with everyone quickly, pose for a good picture, and let one of the PR team hand the family a pre-signed 8x10 of Gutsy. The hold up was Cloudy, who took the time to say hello to everyone, to talk to them, and even personalize autographs on whatever people wanted signed. He signed jerseys, and hockey sticks, and action figures, and playing cards.

At a certain point, the line was held up, and Shannon took it on herself to walk over and poke some fun at Cloudy while she waited.

Or at least, he hoped it was Shannon, that she was in control of Gutsy. He remembered his own experience, of aiming for her head with the t-shirt cannon. He hadn't done that. Gutsy had done that. But still, it was innocuous enough, with Gutsy grabbing some markers from Cloudy's table, and moving them around, or stealing them. To entertain the crowd while they waited.

And it made sense. But Tom only thought of Gutsy, covered in blood, feasting on intestines.

Every time a child ran up to Gutsy, and hugged him, all Tom could see was Gutsy feasting on the kid. Ripping the little child apart, blood and gore everywhere, before swallowing it whole, its body torn into pieces, screams of horror as Gutsy filled the well.

He blinked the sights away, but still they lingered. He had watched the murder last night, and there was nothing that would remove it from his mind.

Tom had seen the news this morning, probably the same coverage his mother watched. They covered the homicide, another in the series, over a dozen dead now, all of them murdered brutally. This thing, that hugged children, and messed around with their parents, had done it. Gutsy had ripped some poor man apart, and he would do it again if they weren't careful.

A child suddenly sprinted to the front of the line, and before anyone could intercept him, whacked Shannon in the leg with a short stick he had found in the parking lot.

Tom watched it happen in slow motion, the child rearing back with the stick and hitting Gutsy in the leg. There was little padding there, only a minor bit of fur, and it looked like it hurt.

Tom saw it all. Saw the rage overcome Gutsy, saw the fury in his eyes reflected in his actions, as he plucked the small child up in one red hand by the skull, and squeezed until its head exploded in an explosion of bone and brain matter. He lifted the kid up and opened his massive black maw, the void where fabric normally was now only filled with darkness, and he swallowed the child whole as the crowd screamed in horror.

But then Tom blinked, and no, Gutsy did nothing. He didn't react to the toddler, who looked at the scary-looking muppet, and then retreated to the line, with a few members of the crowd chuckling. Gutsy didn't react at all to the attack, even if it looked like it hurt.

Tom shook his head again. Shannon was in control.

The day continued, and with only a couple hundred people there, they moved through the queue quickly. Soon, they were done, back in the van, and then back at the arena, packing up the Gutsy costume.

"How you feeling?" asked Tom.

"Tired," said Shannon. "I never got back to sleep last night."

"Neither did I," said Tom.

"Yeah, but I didn't drink a pot of coffee," said Shannon. "I'm fine. It's normal tired. I didn't feel anything from Gutsy. I think we're in the clear."

"You don't feel different? When that kid ran up and whacked you—"

"That happens all the time. The kids don't realize there's a person inside, even worse than the adults. They think I'm some big, invincible monster. So they'll punch you, kick you—"

"I know, but after last night, I only envisioned the worst—"

"When I'm in there, I'm in control," said Shannon. "It took me some time, and some help, but I don't let the suit control my emotions. I control my emotions."

Tom sighed. "I can't help but think—"

"I know. But that's what I'm saying," she said. "We can manage it. You'll see, as you get better control. It'll be okay."

"If you say so," said Tom.

"No anger, no rage," said Shannon. "We keep Gutsy calm, and he'll stay asleep. No more murders."

14

Shannon was wrong. Tom was in the Red again.

He collapsed immediately when he got home, exhaustion hitting him hard. He'd had stressful days—and nights—and had almost no sleep for 48 hours.

Visions of blood and Gutsy still lingered in his mind, but he pushed them away, and this time his weariness was too much, and he fell asleep as soon as his head hit the pillow.

The worry of a Red nightmare hadn't crossed his mind. Shannon had been right, he was sure she was, but he closed his eyes and the next thing he saw was a world in red.

No, no, this isn't right. Shannon had said we can control him. Shannon had said we can manage him—

But Shannon had been wrong, oh so wrong. Because Tom was trapped in the Red again, and the hunger, the need, was stronger than ever. It overwhelmed everything, and any inner dissent he had, the overwhelming strength of that hunger immediately crushed it.

The craving for blood, for pain, for *chaos*.

He rode through the Red, through Gutsy's vision of the world, and saw it how Gutsy did. He saw the world as an array of targets, as a buffet line, everything categorized at its lowest point as to how many calories would it provide, how much fuel would it give.

How much would it fill the well?

Tom dwelled in that hunger, in this mysterious connection with Gutsy, and he felt a tug, a pull, a feeling of emptiness. A feeling that hinted at something old, something lost, something that had been found, over and over again, but then was lost, expended, and must be done again. Repeatedly, until the universe died.

It was a feeling so big, and so vacuous, that Tom almost was lost in it, but the Red brought him back, the terrible hunger, the search for prey.

Because that was what Gutsy was doing, once again. Searching for someone to destroy, to rip into pieces, and to devour. The dread of it was there in Tom, a feeling he was sure Gutsy didn't feel. He knew he was still in bed, asleep. Did Gutsy feel his presence? Did Gutsy know he was there?

Tom didn't know, but he knew Gutsy didn't feel dread for the hunt. The hunger said otherwise. Gutsy was ready, and he moved with the same assured purpose as he had the night before, except this time, Tom was a passenger once again.

Gutsy moved down the street, slipping between the shadows, along the nooks and crannies of the buildings, avoiding all the eyes of the hundreds if not thousands of people who crossed his path. Buildings and streets and cars and people moved inside the Red, and Tom grew accustomed to it, and started to pick everything out.

He recognized the bars, the restaurants. The people stood out, splotches of red, but everything had a distinction here, when he knew how to look. It felt like when he was a child, and he solved a seeing-eye puzzle. He saw the landmarks as they moved. He knew where Gutsy moved, even as Gutsy jumped between shadows and out of eye lines.

But above all else, there was the hunger. It drove Gutsy. That bottomless well that needed to be filled. It was so strong, such a great need, a need that Tom had never felt so strongly in his entire life. He wasn't an addict, and had never faced such a terrible yearning. Even so, he doubted any human was capable of such a feeling, because their appetite would never be as demanding as Gutsy's.

Tom felt that well, felt it like he would feel his own stomach, right before dinner, after a long day, his stomach grumbling even as he boiled the macaroni for his dinner. He saw it, and he had thought it bottomless. An infinite vacuum that Gutsy merely poured whatever he found into, whatever poor victim he could rip apart and devour.

But it wasn't endless, wasn't bottomless. There was a bottom, and it had filled.

Where are we going?

With an understanding of Gutsy's vision, Tom now could track his movement from within his nightmare. They were moving past the bars and restaurants. They passed hundreds and hundreds of people. Red splotches in a red sea, the potentiality of death and chaos measured in the scale of crimson.

All of them were targets, all of them were food. But Gutsy didn't look in their direction. They were all noise, distraction.

But now, Gutsy moved past the crowded areas around the bars, and into the more residential area, farther from downtown.

He'd never gone this far before. He's growing stronger.

This is where the high rises were, the looming condos and apartments, for all the movers and shakers who worked downtown, or those with the money and capital to afford an apartment that cost $5000 a month.

Gutsy didn't want them. He had a target in mind.

But who?

Tom remembered Sam, and the anger and vengeance that Gutsy had felt as he targeted him, isolating him and singling him off to kill him in an alley. But who had angered him? Who had attacked him?

The child.

But the kid had hit him out in the suburbs. Surely the kid's family didn't live downtown, did they?

Tom didn't know, but he'd been with Shannon the entire time with Gutsy, and he had watched him like a hawk. There had been no other outright antagonism.

Maybe the kid's family lived here. And what better way to quench that thirst, to feed that hunger, and to cause as much chaos as possible but to brutally dismember a small child, before feasting on his guts?

This sparked an even deeper dread in Tom, and he desperately wanted to wake up, *please, I don't want to see this,* but he was in prison here, in this nightmare. Only Gutsy's mind could let him go, and it was a steel trap.

Gutsy moved, his vision moving through the red, and Tom knew this area less. He had only driven through it, never bothering to stop in the wealthy area. Just existing here cost more money than he had.

But Gutsy advanced, even as Tom's dread built. He didn't want to watch a child be killed, and he couldn't shut his eyes here. He only hoped his nightmare would end before the killing blow, so he could at least feel the guilt without the accompanying vision of murder.

The Red shifted, and Gutsy stood in front of a high rise, a new condominium, thirty stories tall, a modern building with sharp angles of metal and glass. Gutsy moved toward it and then he was inside, and he jumped quickly now in the well lit lobby, avoiding security cameras, the guard who manned the front desk, the young woman walking her small dog out front. Gutsy slithered around their vision effortlessly, and then he was in the elevator, and then he was moving up.

Tom couldn't make out the floor they were headed to, but Gutsy stood in the elevator, motionless, waiting. His target was close now, and the gnawing hunger and excited appetite were all Tom felt, the dread all gone, all feelings gone, all he felt was Gutsy, it was too much, too much for any human to feel.

The elevator dinged, and Gutsy stepped out, moving quickly, and now Tom saw Gutsy's prey, a massive red splotch, through walls, through doors, a huge splash of crimson that vibrated and glowed in Gutsy's vision. In his short time sharing Gutsy's perspective, he had seen nothing like it. It stood out more than anyone or anything, and now he knew.

He knew why Gutsy had moved so far afield from his base, and why Gutsy had targeted this person.

What caused chaos, and what caused pain?

Change. Abrupt change, without planning or thought of circumstance. Gutsy inflicted abrupt, horrible violence, that shocked, not only in its brutality, but in its pointlessness. Gutsy wanted anarchy and fear. How do you inspire fear?

By targeting those who feel invincible.

Gutsy moved toward his prey. Tom realized now they were in the penthouse, which cost at least a few million alone. He didn't stop, and he didn't slow, not yet. They were alone with the target, Gutsy and his gazelle.

The world was dark, but Gutsy only saw the field of red, and his victim, the bright red splotch within it. Tom realized the man was asleep, and Gutsy moved through the penthouse, until he stood in the bedroom, at the foot of the bed. Then he stopped, and he waited.

This was when Tom would wake up. He wouldn't see the death blow or the gore. He'd wake up, and turn on the news, and he would get a call from his mother, asking about the terrible killer that was loose in his city, and if he was okay, and she would tell him how worried she was.

But Tom didn't wake up. He stayed in the Red, and watched as the man awoke, unsure of what he saw looming at the edge of his bed. The man would reach for his phone, and turn on his flashlight, and see Gutsy standing there, bathed in red, hovering over him, silently. The man would yell at first, confused, but then Gutsy would reach for him, and lock his red right hand around the man's ankle, and he would squeeze, until all the bones in his leg were shattered.

Tom didn't wake up.

Instead, he watched as Gutsy ripped Jeremy Becker apart. He ripped him limb from limb, his legs first, and then his arms. Jeremy was conscious for all but his left.

Tom didn't wake up after Jeremy died, which was shortly thereafter.

Tom only woke after Gutsy had pulled Jeremy apart, and ate everything but his bones.

15

"You said we could manage it!"

"I thought we could," said Shannon. She paced back and forth in the break room. "I didn't feel anything strange yesterday."

"Gutsy killed Jeremy Becker. I watched it happen, through his eyes. God almighty—" but then the thought overwhelmed Tom. He had woken up after the nightmare, early in the morning, already exhausted, and he hadn't gone back to sleep. He had called Shannon and told her to meet him at the arena.

Gutsy had already returned to his normal location, without a spot of blood or gore on him. It was impossible. He had cleaned the flesh from Jeremy's bones, like he was eating fried chicken wings. Tom saw it all, felt it all, and he did all he could to keep it from his mind now.

Worse than anything, worse still was that he had felt Gutsy's relief as he swallowed Jeremy's flesh. He had felt the well fill, and the terrible hunger subside. He had felt the meat slide into that dark void inside of Gutsy—

"What do we do?" asked Shannon.

"We destroy him," said Tom. "There are no other options. We obviously can't manage him. His hunger clearly isn't predicated on the whims of our emotions, or on petty vengeance."

"Why would he go after Becker?" asked Shannon. "He was just some guy at the event. Hell, he left after his speech. We were in one photo together, and then he was gone."

Tom thought to Gutsy's perspective. To the bright scarlet splotch in the sea of Red that was his gaze.

"Chaos, Shannon," said Tom. "Becker screamed as he was killed, but he doesn't feel any more pain than any one else. But he's rich. He's a millionaire. What will happen now that he's dead?"

"I don't know," said Shannon. "His kids will be a little bit richer."

"Maybe," said Tom. "Or maybe the stock price will fall, and people will fight for control of his business, and stores will close, and even more people will lose their jobs, people who can't afford it. It's a ripple effect. It's not just what slides down his gullet. It all helps fill the well."

"How do you know that?"

"I don't know," said Tom. "I just sense it in my nightmares."

"Did you sense anything else?"

Tom searched back through his hazy memory. "It's hard

to tell. So much of it gets washed away when I wake up. I remember the broad strokes, but the finer details are harder to place. But it's getting easier to remember. I don't know what that means, but I don't like it. I don't want to get any closer to that thing."

"You said fill the well," said Shannon. "What does that mean?"

"I don't know," said Tom. "Maybe it's just my creative writing classes coming back. But I don't have to reach for that phrase. It's right there, when I need to describe how Gutsy works. He doesn't have a stomach. He doesn't work like us. There's some void inside, that he's trying to fill. The bigger the target, the more blood, the more pain, the more chaos—the more it fills."

Shannon turned and stared at him. "What happens when he fills that void?"

"I don't know," said Tom. "I don't want to find out. That's why we have to destroy it."

Shannon took a deep breath. "I don't know—"

"What else can we do?" asked Tom. "I can't stand by and watch it kill more people without trying to stop him."

"Do we even know if he can be destroyed?"

"It's just fur and cloth and foam."

"It is right now," said Shannon. "But whatever he turns into when he wakes up, it isn't cloth. It's flesh, some sort of flesh."

"Well, he's asleep now," said Tom. "We *can* burn cloth."

"You want to burn him?"

"I think it's the best way," said Tom. "Down to ashes. And then spread them. Take no chances. Maybe that will be the end."

"They'll see us take the costume out of the arena."

"I don't care at this point," said Tom. "They can fire me. If it means I lose the job, so be it."

"I—"

"You can find more work," said Tom. "Your mom will be okay."

"It's not just that," said Shannon. "Doing this, it's not just about losing our job. It's about—about angering him. What if—"

"What if it doesn't work?"

"Yes," said Shannon. "Because you've felt him when he was angry."

"I have," said Tom. He remembered the raw anger. The rage. It was overpowering. It filled his entire body, and the only thing that quenched it was bloodshed.

"If we try and destroy it, and we fail," said Shannon. "I don't think Gutsy will take it lightly. We might be the next targets."

"He needs us," said Tom.

"Does he, though?" asked Shannon. "Now that he's so popular, the team will always hire more people to 'play' him. There will always be more grist for the mill."

"We have to try."

"You're willing to take the risk?"

"Yes."

"Okay then," said Shannon. She took another deep breath. "How do you want to do it?"

Tom looked at her. "I don't know what Gutsy is," he said. "But everything burns."

*

They stood in an abandoned lot near the arena. They had found an empty burn barrel, left behind by some homeless people. It was blackened and charred, but was still whole, and would withstand any fire they could set. It was hours until dawn.

Shannon held Gutsy in her arms. The leggings, the bulbous torso, and finally, Gutsy's massive head.

"Dump them," said Tom, and Shannon dropped them all into the barrel.

Tom carried the can of gasoline. He had stopped at a gas station on the way to the arena. He knew they would need it. Even if Shannon had said no—he would have done it himself.

He popped the cap and dumped the entire gallon into the barrel, soaking Gutsy through. The foam, the fur, the cloth that made him all soaked through with accelerant. When they lit, he would burn up in seconds.

"Are we sure we want to do this?" asked Shannon. "If—"

"Can you take another death on your conscience?" asked Tom. "I can't."

Shannon stared at the barrel, a part of the suit still sticking out, and then looked at Tom, and nodded. Tom grabbed the book of matches from his pocket and struck one, the piece of wood flaring up.

He watched it ignite and solidify into a flame.

"Back up," said Tom. Shannon took a couple steps back, and then Tom dropped the match into the barrel, and quickly jumped back.

The fire hit the gasoline, and the barrel ignited with a WHOOMPH in a flash. The flames licked up into the sky at first and then settled into a more steady flame. Tom heard the sounds of ignition, as the various parts of Gutsy lit on fire, and then burned to nothing.

"God, what's that smell?" asked Shannon.

Tom took a small whiff, just a slight inhalation, and he immediately understood what Shannon meant. He had expected some weird smells, as the foam pieces and plastic bits burned, but this was something entirely different.

Tom had worked as a roofer, briefly, before he threw his back out, only a week into the job. They had to lay down tar on one of the commercial jobs, and it smelled brutal, and dark, and awful, and the stench had stuck to him for days after, no amount of showers getting the stink off him.

But truly, the smell wasn't tar. It wasn't anything Tom had ever smelled before, a combination of rotten eggs, of sulfur, and tar, and a thousand other sour smelling chemicals he'd briefly encountered throughout his life.

"Don't breathe it in," said Tom. "Maybe it's the glue they used for the suit, or something."

"I don't think so," said Shannon. "I don't think it's the glue."

"Then what could it be?" asked Tom, but Shannon didn't answer. She only stared at the barrel. The fire had smoldered down a little, as the contents of the barrel had burned. There was much less Gutsy than there used to be.

Tom covered his mouth and nose and peeked over the edge. There wasn't much left. The leggings were gone, and the bulbous torso had melted down into sludge. Only the head was left, partially, a single angry eye of Gutsy staring up. It didn't move.

Tom grabbed the can of gasoline and upended it, a slight bit remaining in the bottom of the container. It instantly ignited the fire remaining, and he stepped back. The scent was still there, still terrible, and he stepped back even farther. He didn't want to smell it. Shannon only stared at the barrel, her eyes full of fear and apprehension.

Minutes passed, and the fire burned down again. Tom peeked over the edge, hazarding a look.

There was nothing in the bottom but ashes. After twenty minutes of fire, the suit was gone. The anxiety, the worry, the dread that had festered in the bottom of Tom's guts eased, and he could breathe again.

"Is he gone?" asked Shannon.

"Look for yourself," said Tom, and Shannon peeked in.

"Oh, thank god," said Shannon. "I thought—I thought—"

"You thought the fire wouldn't do anything," said Tom. "Whatever he was, he wasn't invincible. I've got a shovel in my car. We can get it, dig out the ashes, and spread them far and wide. And that'll be the end of it." Shannon only nodded, her eyes still lingering on the barrel, finally breaking away, and then walking with Tom.

She took a deep breath. "Thank you," said Shannon. "Thank you for pushing for it. I was so afraid."

"It—it's okay. It's over now," said Tom. "We'll see if the arena notices it missing."

"Yeah, I hope—"

Where are you going?

Tom jumped at the sound, and Shannon grabbed his arm out of shock. They both froze, and then slowly turned back to the barrel.

Tom remembered, remembered Gutsy moving through the shadows, and creeping, crawling movement that didn't make sense, that ignored the rules of physics.

They both stared as the ashes floated out from the bottom, out of the barrel, and coalesced, the black ash forming first into a blob, floating in the air, softly settling on the ground in front of them. They poured out, slowly at first, but then gained speed, connecting to itself, a wet, black, mess, that squelched and splorched as it formed together again.

It solidified, and then Tom saw the color change, from black to red, the identifiable red of Gutsy. It formed from the bottom up, his feet first, up his long, skinny, furry legs. Then the bulbous torso, that Tom had pelvic thrusted in at his audition. Finally, the neck, and head, the largest part of the suit, looming over both of them, only five feet in front of them. The black ash poured out of the barrel, floating up, a river of ash forming into a river of sludge, piling into the shape of Gutsy, solidifying.

Soon, Gutsy was whole again, the last thing forming being his eyes, his angry, rage filled eyes, always filled with anger. He stared at them, with nothing, empty. The ashen flow had ceased. He was whole again.

He stared at them. The dark, slithering voice emerged from him, his mouth not moving.

It is time we talked.

16

Gutsy stared at them, his hollow, angry eyes pointed at them, standing over them. A cavernous voice emerged from him, his mouth still, a dark voice, a slithering sound that echoed from within his body. It cut straight to Tom's heart. His hair stood on end.

I didn't want to reveal myself. You have forced my hand.

"We—"

Silence.

Gutsy stood motionless, and the voice emerged, but Tom felt the menace, the danger. He remembered the horrible violence that Gutsy had inflicted on each of his victims, and he felt the implicit threat in every word that emerged from him.

I thought we had come to an understanding. It is clear I

was mistaken.

Silence hung between them.

Shannon. We had an agreement.

"I—I don't know what you're talking about," said Shannon.

"What the hell is he—"

Silence. You will know when I am speaking to you.

"I didn't agree to anything," said Shannon.

You wore the suit. You taught me. You stood aside. You understood.

"Understood what?" asked Shannon. "I didn't—"

Another silence, as Gutsy considered them. Tom's guts ached, and he felt the sweat soak his clothes underneath his jacket. Even in the bitter chill, he sweated.

Hmm. I still have much to learn.

"I don't—"

You wore the suit, Shannon. Everything I know of this world is from you. You stayed, when others left. You persevered, when others quit. You did not interfere. I let you continue with your life.

Shannon stared at Gutsy. "I—I needed the money," she said. "I thought you would only kill people if I got angry, or someone made you angry—"

And then a sound emerged from Gutsy, something awful, something terrible, a rattling noise, a dark noise that was unrecognizable as speech. And then Tom realized what it was.

Laughter. It was Gutsy trying to laugh.

I am glad I was summoned to this world. It is the first with the concept of humor. It pleases me.

"You think this is funny?" asked Tom, anger suddenly in

his heart. The words were out of his mouth before he realized his mistake. Gutsy moved then, swiftly, right in front of him, the distance traveled without being seen.

Do not question me.

Tom backed away, and then fell, stumbling backwards. He scrambled to his feet.

Gutsy turned to Shannon, again.

I must feed. It is simple fact. I must build my strength. Death, as you call it, is the most efficient solution. The feelings created—they provide sustenance. You do not control me, Shannon. Any correlation you have witnessed is accidental.

"You can't keep killing people," said Shannon. "These people are suffering. What you're doing—it's awful."

I don't think you can appeal to his sympathy, Shannon. Tom wanted to grab Shannon, and simply run, but he stood motionless. They were here on Gutsy's terms.

Meaningless. They are fuel. I must rebuild my strength. The travel here was draining. Your suffering, your pain—it is what I require. So I take it.

"Please," said Shannon. "Please, you can't—"

Shannon. We share a bond. Do not mistake it for kinship. Limit me and be destroyed. I take no pleasure—

"Don't lie," said Tom. His anger rose again. "You like it. You like their suffering, you like their pain—"

And then Gutsy was there, on top of him, and Gutsy's hand was wrapped around his throat. Tom couldn't breathe, and Gutsy lifted him into the air, holding him there.

I'm going to die, I'm going to die, I can't breathe

You do not question me. Another interruption and I will rip you apart without a thought.

Gutsy dropped Tom, and Tom fell to the ground, coughing, trying to reclaim his breath. Air came into heaving lungs, and Tom could breathe again. He scrambled away from Gutsy, who turned back to Shannon.

I cannot help what I am. This will be your only warning. This—burning—what you did to me. It was draining. I did not enjoy it. Any further attempts to destroy me will lead to punishment. Will lead to more death. The blood will be on your hands.

"We just want the bloodshed to stop," said Shannon.

Impossible. It is the only way.

"We'll quit," said Tom. "We'll quit, and you'll have to bond with new people." Tom winced, expecting Gutsy to attack him again.

No, you will not. You will continue wearing the suit. I require it. Shannon, especially. We will continue this relationship.

"Why should we?" asked Shannon. "You only hurt us."

Because it is what I require. We will not speak again.

"Wait," said Shannon. "Wait. Please. Can I ask you a question?"

Silence, again. Gutsy stood silent, and after a pregnant pause, finally answered.

You may ask me one.

Shannon thought for a moment, and then spoke.

"What are you?"

Gutsy stood there, and Tom thought for a moment that he wouldn't answer. That he would merely disappear. But then he spoke.

I learned your language from you, Shannon. You do not have words for what I am. I am from another place. I was summoned here, and took this form. I am greater than you.

I am beyond you. If I spoke my true language, your minds would reel. Your world will serve my needs. I will rebuild my strength, and continue my purpose. Leave me to my appetite, and you will suffer less. Now, take me back, and leave me. This will be our last conversation.

And then Gutsy was just the suit again, piled on the ground. Whatever force that animated it and made it flesh and blood had left. Gutsy was inanimate again.

They both looked at it, Gutsy's angry eyes staring back.

Tom let out a long breath. Shannon turned and looked at him, and he stared back. Shannon's eyes were filled with fear.

She glanced back at the suit.

"Please, one more question," she said.

There was nothing, no answer.

"I don't think he wants to talk to us anymore," said Tom. "What do we do?"

"We do what he told us to, Tom," said Shannon. "We take him back to the arena, and we leave him alone."

They grabbed the costume, and they walked back. Shannon carried the head, while Tom held the leggings and body. Just touching it made him feel sick to his stomach.

But he would have to wear the suit again. He knew he would. Because they had no other choice. He didn't think Gutsy had told them the entire truth. He felt like it had left out certain facts, and outright lied at other points, but it certainly hadn't lied when it said it was beyond them.

They had set Gutsy on fire. They had burned him to ashes, and he had reformed. He had decided that he would not stay ashes, and thus, he wasn't anymore. Something that powerful—it was on the scale of a demigod. They couldn't compete.

He said none of this. If he was going to talk to Shannon about Gutsy, it would be out of earshot of the suit. He didn't know if the suit heard them when it was asleep, but he wasn't taking chances, not anymore. If they would ever get out from under its control, and truly destroy it, they would have to keep all their secrets as quiet as they could.

They returned to the arena, going back the same way they left. Security didn't stop them, or even see them. The arena was as quiet as a grave. Tom and Shannon returned the suit to its proper location, in the storage closet it was normally kept.

"There," said Tom. "Let's get the hell out of here."

Shannon paused, staring at the suit.

"Shannon," said Tom. "We can't—"

"You said we shared a bond," said Shannon. "Let me ask another question."

The suit only stared ahead, no movement or noise.

"I don't think he's in there right now," said Tom. "I can't stay here any longer, I'm so tired—"

Shannon ignored him. "You said you were from another place. Where is it?"

"Shannon, he's not going to answer. You're only going to make him mad again—"

Gutsy's voice cut through Tom's.

You have no words for my origin. Only one comes close. That word is Hell.

17

They didn't talk about it, not at first.

Both of them were shell-shocked, exhausted, and frankly, traumatized.

They were still in the middle of a road trip, with the team away, and there were no more off-site events in the interim. Gutsy got a break, and by extension, so did they.

Tom slept, finally, collapsing in the early morning after Gutsy spoke to them.

He didn't know if he would sleep. Didn't know if he was capable, anymore. His mind only focused on the nightmares. On the memory of watching whatever Gutsy was re-form into shape. Of him choking Tom on a whim.

But his body was tired, so tired, and eventually he slept, slept without nightmares. He slept for sixteen hours that first night, through most of the day, waking up with the sun already down.

He texted Shannon.

You awake?

She answered. *Yeah*

Want to get a drink?

Sure. As long as it's not downtown.

Tom sent her a bar he went to, The Night Owl, a neighborhood bar far from downtown, and Shannon met him there an hour later. She was already nursing a beer when he arrived. He sat next to her.

"What are you drinking?" he asked.

"An IPA the bartender recommended. I don't remember the name," said Shannon.

"Ah," said Tom. "Not a fan of IPAs."

"Everything else is just drinking water."

Tom ordered a whiskey sour. He took a sip. They had made it strong. He wasn't upset. Right now, he was happy for the booze.

They sat there together, drinking, quiet. The bar was mostly empty, and they sat.

"He didn't kill anyone else last night," said Tom.

"No, I don't think so," said Shannon. "I think he's stayed put."

"We can't just let him keep killing people."

Shannon sighed, and took a long swig of beer, swallowed, and then said nothing.

"What?" asked Tom.

"He could have killed us, Tom," said Shannon. "Like snapping his fingers. You're lucky he didn't choke you to death."

"I'm lucky?" asked Tom. "Yeah, really lucky. I'm a slave to some killer hockey mascot from Hell, and I'm lucky."

"I was worried he'd be invincible. I knew it, I knew it—"

"You didn't stop me," said Tom. "You wanted me to do it. Just because I had the guts to do it—"

"There's a very thin line between brave and stupid," said Shannon. "I let you do it because I hate this, Tom. I do. I hate my job. I hate Gutsy. I hate that I have to do this just to take care of my mom. But I didn't choose this."

"We have a choice in letting him loose and turning a blind eye," said Tom.

"Do we?" asked Shannon. "You tell me. Spell out how we stop him. Tell me your plan."

"There has to be a way," said Tom. "Nothing is invincible. Nothing is unstoppable. Everything has a weak point."

"That's not true," said Shannon.

"Yes, it is, we can—"

"Do you feel upset when someone is struck by lightning?" asked Shannon.

"What?"

"Answer the question. When lightning kills someone. When a tornado blows through and senselessly kills a dozen people in the midwest. When a hurricane storms through Florida."

"I mean, I don't like it," said Tom. "It is upsetting, especially as I've gotten older."

"But do you go on a crusade to stop hurricanes? Do you structure your life around ending tornadoes? Do you declare war on lightning?"

Tom said nothing.

"I don't believe in god," said Shannon. "But I do believe in nature. I believe in luck, and random chance. I believe in chaos. I believe in forces greater than myself. And that is what Gutsy is. I have no fucking clue if what he told us is true. After thinking about it, it might just be a scare tactic, to keep us in line. But his strength is not in doubt. I watched him burn down to ashes, and watched him come back. He's killed over a dozen people, left no evidence, and been seen zero times by people who aren't us. He wasn't lying when he said he was beyond us. I don't know what he is, but we cannot stop him. He can kill us at literally any moment."

"He said you had a bond with him," said Tom.

"Yeah, he thinks I'm his fucking mother or something," said Shannon. "I guess it makes sense, in retrospect. It's why he was so quiet at first. He was learning from me every time I put on the suit. He was figuring out what the world was, how to speak English, how we worked. But now he has all that. I don't think he needs me anymore, not really. I don't paint Gutsy as very sentimental."

"He definitely enjoys the pain. I mean, I enjoy eating a

juicy cheeseburger."

"Yeah, but you don't enjoy slaughtering the cow," said Shannon. "It's a different thing entirely."

"Then what do we do?"

"We keep our heads down."

"And ignore all the people dying?"

"We can't stop him."

"There has to be a way," said Tom.

"You keep saying that," said Shannon. "Show me a plan, and I'll entertain it."

*

Tom knocked on Barbara's open door. She sat at her desk, staring at her computer.

"Hi, Barbara, do you have a moment?"

Oh, hi Tom," she said, her smile appearing in a flash. "I have a couple minutes. How can I help?"

"Do you have the name of Gutsy's designer?"

Barbara looked at him with confusion.

"Why?"

"Oh, some of the fur on Gutsy was coming loose. Shannon had told me the suit just got dropped off by him, or something."

"Yeah," said Barbara. "We never could explain it. But it worked, obviously. You're saying he's falling apart?"

"It's nothing terrible, but we just wanted to know what to replace it with. Figured he would know, if he designed it. He could at least point us toward whoever made the suit."

"Oh," said Barbara. "Well, sure. Give me a second." She clicked through her computer for a few minutes, and then she pulled out a notepad and wrote down some info.

"This is all I have," she said. "Name, number, email. He never got back to me after he dropped off the suit. Maybe you'll have better luck."

Tom took the info and left with a smile, but he didn't have any more luck than Barbara had. The email had no response after a week.

"Hey, this is Claypool. Leave a message," said the voice-mail, short and to the point. Norman Claypool was the man's full name, and a search online brought up his portfolio, which was an assembly of different art installations, some in traditional media, and some not. Tom had no idea why they picked Claypool to design Gutsy, but after reading a few old magazine articles on him, it seemed he was a flash in the pan artist who was hot, and someone, maybe Barbara, had thought they'd get buzz for his design.

But his website wasn't updated, and he hadn't posted anything on social media for six months.

Suspicious.

But another dead end. There was no listed address online.

In the meantime, people kept dying.

All Tom had to do was read the news, and every other day, or every other third day, there'd be a new report. Another brutal death. A random target, senseless. It dominated the news now, even reaching some national spotlight, because of the lack of suspects. When there were this many deaths, usually there was some sort of evidence, eventually. The killer would slip up.

Gutsy didn't have to worry about that.

And downtown traffic had slowed down, even. Still,

there were plenty of targets. Plenty of people who thought they were invincible.

But there were no more nightmares. No more trips through the Red. Tom didn't know why not. Maybe because he hadn't worn the suit in some time. Or because Gutsy didn't want him to. But thankfully, he could sleep again, even started a semi-normal sleep schedule again.

And honestly, it was easy, without the nightmares. If he didn't look at the news, he didn't even know anything was wrong. Shannon's proposition that they follow Gutsy's orders didn't seem so absurd anymore.

He felt bad about it, guilty. But she wasn't wrong. Gutsy was beyond them. What could they do?

*

"It's my turn," said Tom. "I'll wear it."

"I'll do it," said Shannon. "I don't care about turns. I'm still taking the mood stabilizers. I can do it."

"If we're going to do this, you can't always wear it," said Tom. "I have to be able to do it, too. Not to mention I think Skates will notice if you're always wearing it."

"I don't think Skates would care, honestly."

"Doesn't matter," said Tom. "It's my turn. I'm going to wear it."

"You sure?"

"Yes," said Tom. "I'm sure. I can do it. I need to do it."

Tom stared at the head of Gutsy, just like before, but now he knew that there was something there, waiting. But Gutsy didn't betray it now. He stayed asleep, or as asleep as he could be. Could Gutsy wake up while they were inside the suit? If he did, what would happen to the person wearing it?

He didn't know, and he didn't want to find out. He would wear the costume, do his job, and move on with his life. That's what they would have to do until he could figure out a plan to stop the suit for good.

"Help me with his head," said Tom, and Shannon helped slide on the Gutsy head, and it was even easier this time. Every time was easier, and Tom hated it.

"Let's get to work," said Tom.

The Brawlers had another home stand, a rough stretch of five games in seven days, maybe the hardest part of their season, and it was back to work for both him and Shannon. Back into the suit.

They went out into the concourse and followed their normal routine. Tom had been nervous all day, and had slept poorly the night before, and had even considered getting sleeping pills, but no, he wouldn't do what Shannon did. He would find a way out of this that wasn't medication. He'd been tense all day, and amping himself up to put on the suit had taken an hour, but he had done it.

But now that the costume was on—it was easy.

Too easy.

It felt good in there. He hated it, but it felt great. Better than it ever had.

It had always felt right, after he got into the suit, and before, he hadn't known why. He knew why now. He knew that what he felt around him was the power of Gutsy. That strength that Gutsy had referenced, the ability, the invincibility. It was there, and even though Tom couldn't access it directly, it was still close by, and through osmosis, made *him* feel better. Feel stronger.

And he kept expecting the evening to go downhill. As he went through photo ops, and different bits with the crowd, and the big skit of the night, he expected Gutsy's overpowering rage to overcome him, to take him over, to fill him with that terrible fury, and presage another gruesome death that night.

But nothing happened. It was just another night in the suit. Sure, there were some drunk people that were a little too handsy. A couple kids bawled their eyes out when they saw him. An opposing fan even started yelling when Gutsy threw his hat, but that had been the end of it.

No explosions of rage. No assaults. No attempts to decapitate Shannon.

He didn't know if it made it better or worse. Was Gutsy trying to manipulate them? Giving them a nicer experience in the suit, so they would play ball with him, and look the other way while he built his strength?

Or was that strength the reason the suit didn't bother him anymore? Had Gutsy fed enough that the side effects wouldn't hurt them anymore?

Tom didn't know, but despite everything going well, it still dominated his mind as the night wore on. The Brawlers were winning in a rout, and Gutsy was out in full force, with the crowd going crazy for him.

"It's time for a GUTSY DANCE PARTY!" yelled the announcer over the PA, and then Tom danced, some of the Ice Girls dancing with him, as the PA pumped out bass heavy music. It was barely dancing on his part, the Gutsy suit not really equipped to do anything but the bare minimum of dancing.

The stadium thumped, with red lights pulsating during

the break. Soon the third period would start up, and Tom could call it for the night, he was tired, and ready to get out of the suit without incident—

Then the red lights shone in his eyes again, and the vision overtook him.

It was alien, what he saw.

He was in the Red again, seeing through Gutsy's eyes. He had learned to parse through it on Earth, but seeing this place. What was he looking at?

It wasn't human, it wasn't Earth. It was something else entirely.

He moved through it, searching for prey, and that much was familiar. But something was different, aside from the setting.

The hunger. It wasn't there. That desperate need, the urge to fill the well, it was gone. Gutsy's hunger had been slated.

Still, where were they? Was this where Gutsy was from? Was this Gutsy's home?

It didn't seem it. Gutsy moved like a predator. Even more, Tom sensed Gutsy's feelings, and this wasn't home to him. Gutsy felt about this place like he felt about Earth.

A trough. A buffet.

But why did it look like this?

There were no darker splotches in this sea of red. The landscape was different, sure, no buildings, only some sort of protoplasmic plant life, and that sprung from the rocky ground, rocks unlike anything on Earth. It hung in the air as well, and without his own vision, he had no true idea what it looked like. He didn't even know if his human eyes would see it the same way.

But as Gutsy searched for prey, it was clear, there was

none. None within sight. Gutsy hunted, still prowled this alien landscape, but he saw nothing.

Tom realized this was a memory, a distant one. When, he didn't know, but without Shannon's medications, he too had formed a bond with Gutsy, and somehow saw back into Gutsy himself.

And then he realized.

There was no prey here because Gutsy had already fed on it. And he looked over the vast landscape, and he saw other things, and he didn't realize, they weren't red, but they were him as well. Other Gutsies. But they weren't Gutsy here, no, they had another form, another shape, something Tom didn't recognize, and this was all Gutsy did. He moved between worlds. He consumed everything. And then he moved on, someway, somehow.

And then the vision ended, and Tom was dancing, still, and the thumping music ended, and he was done, and he found Shannon, and he followed her out onto the concourse, and then into the back area, and he couldn't get the suit off fast enough, and he put Gutsy away, and then pulled Shannon out of earshot of that thing, and away from Gutsy's closet, out of the break room, down the hall, even.

A stray person wandered by, here and there, but Tom didn't care, he needed to tell Shannon.

"I saw something, Shannon."

"What?" she asked. "Another death?"

"No," he said, and he told her.

"What does that mean?"

"It means that if we just stand back and let him kill—" Tom struggled, bent over, taking a breath. He took a series of them, slowing down his heart rate.

"Are you okay?"

"He'll kill everything, Shannon. When he says rebuild his power, he doesn't mean to be healthy, whatever that means for him. It means enough power to take over."

18

They sat in Shannon's car, parked outside the arena. Tom shivered.

"I'm sorry," said Shannon. "The heat takes forever to get working."

"I'll be fine," said Tom. He rubbed his hands together, and blew in them.

"Are you sure that's what you saw?" asked Shannon.

"Yes," said Tom. "It wasn't even what I saw, really. It's what I *felt*."

"I don't understand."

"I can't explain it," said Tom. "It doesn't make sense, but Gutsy doesn't make sense. Putting on that suit, enough times. I'm connected to him, in a weird way. He talked about your bond, but I'm bonded to him too. I'm not even sure if he realizes it. But I saw his memory. He had hunted a whole world to extinction. Had transformed it, somehow. And there wasn't only one of him. There were many. They were all hunting."

"What did he look like?"

"I don't know," said Tom. "Not like Gutsy. In that place, I don't think seeing worked the same way. I don't think Gutsy cares."

Shannon stared out the windshield, into the cold night. The arena had long since closed, and the fans had either went home, or filtered into downtown.

"I believe you, Tom, I do," said Shannon. "But I still don't know what to do. We can't kill him, we can't. Maybe if we had a nuke or something, that would atomize him, maybe that would do it. Even if we drove him far away, he would just come back. Maybe radiation—"

"I don't have access to radiation," said Tom. "We could maybe break into a hospital and use their X-ray machine, but I don't think that would do it."

"I was thinking more along the lines of uranium, or something," said Shannon. "Like the power core of a nuclear plant."

"Sure as hell can't get that," said Tom. "Wait a minute. Maybe we're thinking about this all wrong."

"What?" asked Shannon. "You have an idea."

"We've been hung up on trying to destroy him," said Tom. "But we don't have to, right?"

"I'm not following," said Shannon.

"He hasn't killed anyone while we're in the suit," said Tom. "It's always after hours. He wakes up, goes out when no one's watching, kills, and then comes back, still in the dark. By daylight, he's always back."

"And?"

"What if we just contain him?" asked Tom. "A cage."

"I don't think a cage will work," said Shannon. "The way he moves, at least when he's alive, it just seems to ignore most laws of physics. It's like he bends with shadows, or something. Clings to walls. Maybe if we had camera footage, we could figure it out—"

"No," said Tom. "Nothing he could see his way out of. Something with no room whatsoever. Airtight. No room to maneuver, no way to get out."

"What the hell would that be?" asked Shannon.

"They make airtight safes," said Tom. "My dad had one."

"Aren't they expensive?" asked Shannon. "Especially something big enough to fit Gutsy in. The leggings fold up, sure, but the torso and head are both gigantic." Shannon looked at him. "But it's not a bad idea. If it's airtight, that'll surely keep him in, right?"

"I don't know what else to do," said Tom. "I think it's worth a shot."

*

"This is the biggest model I've got on premises," said the salesman, standing next to a huge safe, with thick, lead walls. "It weighs almost a ton."

"Airtight, right?" asked Tom.

"Oh, guaranteed. Has a vacuum sealing system that pulls all the air out of the safe. Fireproof, waterproof, and rated to withstand any explosives up to C4. You drop this thing off a building, it'll put a hole in the street."

Tom looked inside. Despite its size, the interior wasn't *that* big. He thought Gutsy would fit if they squeezed the head and torso inside. Barely.

"What do you think?" asked Tom, looking at Shannon.

"I think it's big enough," she said.

"How much?" asked Tom.

"Six thousand," said the salesman. "But I'll tell you what. This model is being discontinued. Nothing wrong with it, just the manufacturer wants to make some style upgrades. If you take it off my hands today, I'll give you fifteen percent off. Makes it just over five grand."

"We'll take it," said Tom. Shannon stared at him, her eyes wide. He handed over his credit card to the salesman, a plain smile on his face. He had just paid off all the debt on the card, months of back-rent, and now he was rocketing right back up to the limit again. He would worry about it later. They had to contain that thing now. Maybe he could get Cloudy to pay this off, too.

"How quickly can you get it delivered?" asked Tom.

"When do you need it?"

Tonight, if possible," said Tom.

"Tonight?" asked the salesman. "Let me call my guy. I might be able to arrange something." He disappeared into his office.

"You just put five thousand dollars on your credit card!" said Shannon, trying to keep her voice low.

"Yeah," said Tom. "I've been in debt before. At least this time it's to save the world—"

"Looks like he can swing it," said the salesman. "He's done for the day. He owes me one. Where do you want it delivered?"

"Do you know where the Brawler's arena is?" asked Tom.

*

"I hope this works," said Tom.

"I hope it does too, considering how much it cost," said Shannon.

They stared at the heavy safe, sitting just outside their small part of the arena. The driver had shown up at the loading dock, and Tom and Shannon had guided him and his forklift and the safe through the arena, to this very spot. With a few words to their friends who worked security, no one stopped them. They worked there, and they sounded confident. That was ninety percent of the battle.

Then Shannon had worked the whole night as Gutsy, as the Brawlers played the second half of a back-to-back. They won again, and the crowd had been raucous. They were playing themselves into the playoffs after a multiple year drought, and everyone was happy.

Shannon reported no strangeness within the costume. No visions, and no mood swings.

Could Gutsy read them? He had said he had learned from Shannon. Could he also learn their plans? Tom hoped not, because he would never let them do this if he did.

"Are you ready?" asked Tom.

"As ready as I'll ever be," said Shannon. They had waited for the arena to clear out, and most of the workers to leave. Their part of the arena was mostly empty anyway, home to the Ice Girls, and them. The Ice Girls were all gone. They should be left alone.

"Let's do it," said Tom, and they walked to Gutsy's closet, where he sat, exactly where Shannon had left him after her shift. They grabbed him, Tom getting his legs and torso, while Shannon took the head.

Would he wake up? If he knew what they were planning, he would.

They moved fast, and piled the legs, torso, and then head into the massive safe. They were bulky, and it was close, but Tom didn't stop to measure, and pushed the big door shut. It was heavy, and maybe it slightly smooshed Gutsy's head, but he didn't care, and he locked it. He pushed the electronic button that enabled the airtight seal, and he heard a small *whoosh* as it sucked all the air out of the safe, leaving it im-penetrable. It was sealed. There was no way in or out.

"—that was easier than I expected," said Shannon.

"I wouldn't call that easy," said Tom. "I'm going to owe that store money for my entire adult life."

"But he didn't wake up, or struggle," said Shannon. "He just let us put him in there."

"I don't think he's always conscious," said Tom. "My guess is he's conserving strength."

"So, what now?" asked Shannon. "Do we just go home?"

"You can," said Tom. "I'm going to stay and watch."

"Watch what?" asked Shannon. "A big safe?"

"I wouldn't be able to sleep at home anyway," said Tom. "I need to know if it works."

"Well, I'm not leaving you here alone."

Tom walked over to the rack of folding chairs nearby, and grabbed two, unfolding one for her, and one for him.

"Then here we'll wait," said Tom.

"How long?"

"He's only attacked at night, so far," said Tom. "So until

dawn. I will have considered this a success if works until dawn."

"Okay, a second question, then. How long will we do this?" asked Shannon. "And how long will it work?"

"If this is what it takes," said Tom. "I'll do this forever. Maybe not stay up all night staring at a locked safe. But locking away that suit every night? That's easy."

"Simple, maybe," said Shannon. "But not easy. You did just go five grand in debt."

"If it saves lives, that's a cheap price."

"If it works."

"It'll work," said Tom. "Why are you so pessimistic? You have to have hope."

"After you hope for a long time, Tom, you start drowning in it. It's easier to just drain the pool."

"I get that," said Tom. "I don't know. I can't live my whole life expecting the worst to happen. There has to be happiness out there, somewhere."

"Happiness is a word for rich people," said Shannon. "For Jeremy Becker. For Cloudy. They can afford it. I can afford it for a few minutes, while I watch TV and eat dinner."

"Well, Becker isn't happy anymore," said Tom. "I'll give Gutsy that. He's equal opportunity. He kills the rich and poor alike."

"Not sure Gutsy is concerned much about capitalism," said Shannon. "Only thing that rings true is us cleaning up the fucking mess while the cops run around doing nothing."

Tom chuckled, and then they settled into silence, staring at the safe. Shannon took out her phone and stared at it, while Tom let his mind wander.

Could he do this forever?

Be the zookeeper for whatever Gutsy was, for the rest of his life? A man-eater, a tiger, that he and Shannon would parade out for hockey fans, and then lock him away at night, so he doesn't kill anymore?

What if they fired him, or Shannon? All it would take is a few new people, and they wouldn't know any of these impossible things that just happened to be true. And Gutsy would get out, and kill again, and grow into whatever he could become. Another job Tom couldn't quit—

Creak

"Did you hear that?" asked Tom.

"Hear what?" asked Shannon, looking up from her phone.

"That noise," said Tom. They sat silently.

"You must be imagining things," said Shannon. "I didn't—"

Creaaaak

"That was it," said Tom. "That definitely came from the safe."

"What do we do?" asked Shannon.

CreeaaaaaaaAAAAAK

"Fucking hell, I don't know," said Tom. "We can shore it up, or something—"

"I'll just take out my welding gear," said Shannon. "What the hell does that mean, shore it up?"

"I'm trying to think—"

BRAAAAAAANG

BRAAAAAAANG

CLAAAAAAANK

CLAAAAAANK

The door to the safe shifted from one side to the other.

Fuck.

Then it fell, straight out, and down, leaving the safe completely open. Gutsy stood, his massive shape halfway out of the safe.

"Shit," said Shannon.

That required significant energy.

"Gutsy, please—" started Shannon.

I told you to stay out of my way. You must be punished.

And then he moved, once, twice, and was gone.

19

Shannon and Tom stared at each other. The door to the safe laid on the floor between them.

"Fuck fuck fuck fuck fuck!" yelled Shannon.

"What the fuck," said Tom. "How the fuck did he do that?"

"He's too strong," said Shannon. "I told you, I told you—"

"What do we do? What do we do?" asked Tom.

"What did he say?" asked Shannon, scrambling. "He said he would punish us. Punish us. What the fuck does that mean? How would he punish us?"

"He—he could go after loved ones," said Tom, quietly. "My mom, she's like a hundred miles away. I don't think—"

"My mom!" said Shannon. "The nursing home is a few miles from here."

"He hasn't gone that far before," said Tom. "He's gone maybe a mile away, into downtown."

"He wants to punish us, Tom," said Shannon. "We have to go stop him. We have to protect her." Shannon started running toward the exit, toward her car. "We can get there before him, if we hurry."

Tom ran after her, trying to keep up. His cardio wasn't as good as hers, and he was already gasping for breath after only a minute of running after her. Shannon pushed through the exit door that led directly to the staff parking lot, and she sprinted toward her car, one of the few cars parked out there.

She jumped into the driver's seat, and he ran behind her, finally getting to the passenger side.

"Get in, get in!" yelled Shannon, already starting up the engine. As soon as he was sitting down she squealed off.

"Jesus, give me a second," said Tom, slamming his door shut and sliding his seatbelt on.

"We don't have time," said Shannon. "He's already moving. We have to beat him there."

Shannon sped out of the parking lot and onto a surface road with barely a glance for oncoming traffic. Tom grabbed a hold of the door handle as the car shifted.

"We can't do anything if we get in a car accident," said Tom.

"I've never been in a car accident," said Shannon, her voice calm as she steered over the surface streets, and then blew through a red light, and then blew through another.

"A fucking cop is going to pull us over."

"Let them try," said Shannon. "That motherfucker isn't getting my mom."

A car honked loudly as Shannon cut them off, her small sedan blazing through the night. The roads were mostly deserted, and she pumped the brakes as she slid through a turn, through yet another red light, and this time another car almost hit them, dodging past them, their horn blaring.

"Fuck you," said Shannon, continuing to go, turning down another side road, this time a one-way road.

"We're going down the wrong way, Shannon."

"It's the fastest way," said Shannon. "Worth the risk."

"I don't know if I can agree with that," said Tom, as they knocked a side-view mirror off a parked car.

"It's only a minute away," she said. "We've had to have beaten him there. We've had to of."

"But what—what do we do?" asked Tom. "We can't stop him. He's stronger than us."

"There are other people there," said Shannon. "He doesn't want witnesses. If other people know about him, it'll keep him from hunting. He'll run. He'll run."

Shannon repeated it, and Tom didn't know if she believed it, or she only wanted to believe it. She accelerated hard as they hit a straightaway, now a few miles from the arena, in an area filled with nursing homes and retirement care facilities. Between them lay doctor's offices, all for senior patients. A cottage industry, taking care of the dying.

"There it is," said Shannon. It looked normal from the outside, a big, brick, single story building. The tires skidded as Shannon took a hard right and pulled into the closest parking spot. She was out of the car before the engine had fully died, sprinting into the home.

Shannon disappeared through the automatic doors, and Tom followed, running as hard as he could. There had to be security here, or some overnight watch. They wouldn't just let Shannon in, would they?

He popped through the front doors and they had a front desk, but the woman staffing it was chasing after Shannon, who was already past her.

"She texted me, Nancy, she texted me, I'm sorry," said Shannon, who continued to sprint.

"Ms. Wood, please, it's too late," said Nancy, a small woman in blue scrubs, who jogged after Shannon. "You can't visit her right now. If there's a problem, our medical staff—"

Shannon didn't answer, and Nancy couldn't keep up. Tom ran after both of them.

All Tom could think was, what if they found Gutsy in there? What could they do to him? He *was* beyond them, and they couldn't stop him, and they couldn't contain him. All of Tom's efforts had proved that true. Shannon had said he would run if there were witnesses. Maybe that was true. Maybe he didn't want to be discovered, at least not yet. But they couldn't watch her mom all the time. They couldn't protect anyone all the time. If Gutsy really wanted to, he would kill whoever he wanted.

But if they found Gutsy in there—would he run?

Or would he just kill all three of them?

Tom had caught up to Shannon as she tried to get inside her mom's room. Nancy had caught up as well. The door was locked, and Shannon was shaking and knocking, trying to get inside.

"Ms. Wood, please," said Nancy. "It's locked. I have the keys. You can't—"

"Please, Nancy, please let me in," said Shannon. "I'm

worried. I need to see her."

"Okay, okay," said Nancy. "Just step back from the door. Let me unlock it. Please be quiet. Everyone is trying to sleep."

Shannon backed away from the door, but Tom saw the tension in her still, and Nancy pulled a keyring from her belt and reflexively went to the right key, unlocking it, and opening it.

"Who are you?" asked Nancy, looking at Tom.

"It's my boyfriend," said Shannon, quickly, and Tom eyed Shannon. She stared back, telling him to *go with it* without saying any words.

Nancy opened the door, and Shannon rushed in. Tom followed behind, his breath held, his heart beating hard, expecting to see Gutsy's massive frame ripping Shannon's poor mother apart. Or just see the remnants of his carnage, a dead body, unrecognizable.

But he followed Shannon in regardless, he would follow her, they were in this together.

But Gutsy wasn't in there. Only Shannon's mom, still laying in bed. She looked up blearily as Nancy turned on a small corner lamp, providing just enough light to see by.

"Shannon?" asked her mother.

"Yes, Mom," said Shannon. "It's me."

"What's happening? Why are you here?" she asked.

"I was worried about you," said Shannon. "I—I had a premonition, and it scared the living hell out of me. I needed to see you."

"Oh—okay," said her mom, laying back in bed. "I'm fine, everything's fine. Come here."

Shannon approached her mother's bed, and they embraced, Shannon burying her face in her mother's shoulder.

"Everything's alright, dear, everything's fine," she said. "Who's this with you?"

"It's my boyfriend, Tom," said Shannon, quickly.

"Oh, how nice," she said. "I'm Mary. Nice to meet you."

"Nice to meet you, too," said Tom, still on edge. Gutsy wouldn't attack now, would he? Not with them there.

"Ms. Wood," said Nancy. "Visiting ended hours ago."

"Can we please stay, Nancy?" asked Shannon. "Please? We'll be quiet. We won't leave the room. We'll be out of here early in the morning. I won't cause any problems. I promise."

Tom looked at Nancy, who was silent, her face unreadable. Then it relented.

"Fine," said Nancy, taking a deep breath. "But you must be quiet. Everyone is trying to sleep. If you're making any noise, I will have to force you to leave."

"Quiet as a mouse," said Shannon, smiling sweetly.

"You okay, Mary?" asked Nancy.

"I'm alright," said Mary. "Glad to see my daughter."

Nancy backed out of the room, shutting the door behind her. She did not lock it.

"Shannon," said Mary. "Is everything okay?"

"I—" started Shannon. "I was just suddenly very worried about you. A bad feeling. I couldn't shake it. I needed to make sure you were okay."

"And that's all it is?" asked Mary.

"Yes," said Shannon. "That's all it is. Staying here with you will make me feel better."

"And you, young man?" asked Mary. "You came out here just because Shannon was worried about me?"

"Well, yeah," said Tom. "It was an easy decision." He smiled as genuinely as he could.

"I'm glad she's with someone who's so supportive," said Mary. "Well, I need to go back to bed."

"Please, sleep, Mom," said Shannon. "We'll take the chairs."

"Will they be comfortable enough?" asked Mary.

"I think so," said Shannon.

Tom looked at the two chairs, both recliners. They would work. He didn't know if he'd be able to sleep.

"You can have that one," said Shannon, and Tom took it without argument. Would they just sit here in the dark?

Shannon turned off the lamp, and then saw there was a nightlight in the corner, enough to see by. Shannon moved to the other recliner.

She pulled her phone out, a slight glow in the dark.

His phone buzzed. He opened it to see a text from her. *He's not here. Do you think he would still come?*

Tom replied. *I don't think so. He would have been here by now.*

I can't leave. Not tonight. Don't know what Gutsy meant, then.

I don't either.

You can sleep, if you want. I'll be awake.

Tom replied with a thumbs up and closed his phone. He reclined his seat back. It was quite comfortable. But he didn't know if he'd be able to sleep.

They sat there in the dark. What the hell had Gutsy meant? He'd punish them? How? Tom wasn't worried about his mother. Gutsy could move quickly, but he couldn't walk a hundred miles in a night. His dad had passed five years ago. He had no other close relatives, and his aunt and cousins lived three states over.

His mind whirled, and looped, and then his eyes closed, and he wouldn't be able to sleep, surely not—

His phone buzzed in his pocket.

BZZZZ BZZZZ BZZZZ

Tom opened his eyes, blinking them open.

What time was it?

Dim sunlight streamed through the windows. The sun was up, just barely. He looked over and saw that both Shannon and Mary were both asleep, both untouched. Gutsy hadn't come here, at least not to kill.

His phone still buzzed in his pocket, and he reached for it, sleepy fingers trying to navigate denim.

Tom looked at the screen. Skates was calling him.

"Hello?" said Tom, trying to sound coherent.

"Sorry for waking you, kid," said Skates, his voice rough.

"It's alright, Skates," said Tom. "What's going on?" Shit, he remembered, they had left the safe. Fuck, they would want to know what the hell had happened. "I—"

"Wait a minute, kid," said Skates. He heard Skates blow his nose. "I gotta tell you something, and it ain't going to be easy."

Fuck, they were getting fired. No, they couldn't, they couldn't unleash Gutsy onto the world.

"Skates, please—"

"No, let me finish, kid," said Skates. "I'll never be able to get it out if you keep stopping me." He paused, and Tom heard him take a deep breath. "The bastard—"

And then Skates stopped, his breath catching, and Tom realized he was crying. Not just crying. Sobbing, on the other end of the line.

"The bastard killed Cloudy," said Skates, forcing the words out. "He killed Cloudy, kid. They found him, his wife, his kids, early this morning. Dead."

20

"No, I've read through the contract," said Tom. "It says specifically, defect or deficiency that leads to undue opening, and guess what happened? The damn thing opened after it was locked. You're damn lucky it didn't have anything valuable in it!"

Tom yelled on the phone. He and Shannon sat in the arena, near the broken safe. They had moved the safe door over to the side. It was slightly less obtrusive there. Very few staff were there. The Brawlers' games were cancelled for the indeterminate future.

"No, I don't want it fixed," said Tom. "I want you to take it away, and give me my money back. It's literally plastered over all your marketing. Money-back guarantee! Are you telling me you're lying to your customers?"

He hadn't wanted to call, but five thousand dollars was a price he would pay if the safe had worked. And maybe the salesman hadn't guaranteed that it would contain Gutsy, but Tom didn't care. And to be frank, anger had built up in him, and he was letting it out.

"Yes, come and get it ASAP," said Tom. "Please, put the money back on the same card. Yes. Yes. Thank you. Bye."

"I don't think I've ever heard you that angry," said Shannon.

"They wouldn't have given me my money back if I didn't get angry," said Tom. "Or maybe they would have, but it would have taken twice as long."

"I'm not arguing with you," said Shannon. Her eyes were red. She had cried at the news, embracing her mother. Cloudy's personal chef had found him and his family dead this morning. They had a house in Federal Hill. The details were ghastly. Cloudy, his wife, his three daughters. All killed. All ripped apart.

They hadn't reported them being eaten, like they hadn't reported it for any of the others, but Tom assumed Gutsy had devoured them.

The whole town was in shock. The mayor had declared it a day of mourning, and the police chief had already had a press conference, declaring a task force to find and apprehend this killer.

But they wouldn't find him. Gutsy left no evidence and no trail.

Tom thought back to the party, where Cloudy had handed him that envelope filled with money. About Cloudy believing in family. About his talk of retiring as a Brawler.

It had come true, at least.

Shannon stared at the ground, her eyes vacant.

"This is our fault," said Shannon.

"We didn't kill him," said Tom. "Gutsy did."

"We provoked him," said Shannon. "We made him angry, and he punished us. You heard him."

"We can't think like that," said Tom. "He's killed before, and he'll kill again, regardless of what we do. The only difference is who he targets. But it's inevitable, Shannon. If he keeps going, he'll get everyone. You, me, your mother, the world. He's a virus. He eats until there's nothing left. We are under no onus to respect him, or to stay out of his way."

"It feels like it's our fault."

"That's what he wants," said Tom. "He understands how to manipulate us. But I'm not going to stop—"

"How you kids doing?" asked Skates as he walked toward them. "Little surprised to see you here."

"We wanted to rehearse a little," said Shannon, glancing at Tom. "Keep our minds off things."

"Yeah," said Skates. "Work always helps keep me focused. I still—I still can't believe it. He was the last guy gone, the last game, like always. We ragged on each other, like we always did." Skates stopped and wiped a tear from his eye. "I've been leaking all day."

"It's hard," said Tom.

"You can say that again, kid," said Skates. "Damn cops. How long? How long has this been going on? Months now, months. Whoever the hell it is, just keeps killing, keeps cutting people into bits. It ain't right. It ain't right. They need to get off their ass and do something. There ain't a man in this world better than Cloudy, and to have that happen to him, and his poor family—" Skates wiped away another tear.

"Whenever they catch 'em, I'd pay good money to get time alone with them. Me, and every guy from the team. There'd be nothing left, that son of a bitch."

"Sorry, Skates," said Shannon. "We can get through this together. Family, like Cloudy always said."

"You're a smart kid," said Skates. "You're right. Family. If you kids need anything, I'll be around. Hell, spend more time here than I do at home." He paused and looked at the safe. "What's this for?"

"Oh, it was for Gutsy," said Tom. "To protect the suit, you know?"

"Oh, I got you," said Skates.

"Safe broke, though. Think they're coming to take it back."

"Can't trust all this modern technology," said Skates. He walked away.

"Have you checked on him?"

"On who? Gutsy?" asked Shannon.

"Yeah," said Tom.

"No," said Shannon. "Why does it—"

Tom went into their office, and then to the utility room door. Shannon was right behind him.

"It's always the same, Tom," said Shannon. "He's always back here."

"I don't trust it, anymore," said Tom. "We have to keep track."

"He always comes back here," said Shannon. "Honestly, I can't even look at him. It makes me sick."

Tom opened the door.

"What the fuck?" asked Tom. Shannon came up next to him, both looking in.

"How the hell—"

Tom had gotten used to finding Gutsy back in the utility closet after his rampages, clean as a whistle, laying exactly as he had when they had put the costume back. But just because he was always there didn't mean that they should assume he would always return.

Today was no different. He had returned to the utility closet after killing Cloudy and his family.

The only thing different was that there were two Gutsy costumes. Identical. Sitting next to each other.

"Uh—"

"How?" asked Tom.

"What did you say?" asked Shannon. "What you told me, the other night? About him replicating? About him taking over?"

"He was weakened. He said so himself," said Tom.

"Cloudy was a public figure. Chaos," said Shannon. "It fed him. And now, with two of him—it'll go even faster."

Tom's heart beat hard in his chest, staring at the leering, dead eyes of two Gutsies, now. He blinked hard, and then shut the door.

"I can't look at them," said Tom. "Not right now." He retreated back out to the safe. Farther from the costumes, the better.

"Jesus," said Shannon.

"There's two of them, now," said Tom.

"It's worse," said Shannon. She stared at him. "Soon there'll be three of them. We have to stop him. I just don't know what to do. We're like ants to him."

"I've been thinking," said Tom.

"Oh no, we're in trouble," said Shannon.

"You're very funny," said Tom. "Comedy genius, even." He paused. "I was thinking, about what Gutsy said."

"When?"

"When he said how he got here. He used the word summoned. He didn't pick Earth. He didn't travel here on his own. Someone pulled him here."

"I didn't take it as that," said Shannon. "I just assumed he didn't really understand the word. God knows how he communicated with other creatures before he got here. If he did it at all. He didn't even know what laughter was."

"Let's take it at face value," said Tom. "If someone pulled him here, who did it?"

"Well, the higher ups hired some artist to design him," said Shannon. "Might be him."

"That's what I thought, too," said Tom. "I tried to hunt him down, but he dropped off the face of the Earth. No social media. No updates on his websites. Just old projects. No answer on his phone or email."

"That's suspicious as hell," said Shannon.

"Yes, but I couldn't find an address," said Tom. "None listed, anywhere, except for some old gallery shows he'd done. Don't know what else to do. I can't *make* him answer his phone."

"Give me a second," said Shannon. "What's his name? His full name."

"Norman Claypool is the name Barbara gave me," said Tom. Shannon started tapping at her phone. "He's done a bunch of different stuff over the years. Some of it looks really cool, and some of it looked like pretentious wankery."

"Claypool? That sounds familiar," said Shannon. She continued to type on her phone.

"What are you doing?"

"I said to give me a second."

"You looking something up?" asked Tom. Shannon didn't answer, not at first. After a few more seconds, she spoke.

"Number 13 Mission Street."

"What's that?"

"Claypool's address."

"How the hell did you find that?"

"Property records are public information," said Shannon. "He didn't bother hiding behind a business or shell account to purchase his property, so I can find it. It's easy. You didn't do that?"

"How the hell would I know how to do that?" asked Tom. "I've never even thought of buying land."

"I used to work in a realtor's office," said Shannon. "We had to do it all the time. You'd be surprised at how many people try to sell a house that isn't theirs."

"Warehouse district?" asked Tom. "I've only driven past it on the interstate."

"It's mostly abandoned buildings at this point. Some artist types have bought up some of it, and made it chic to be there. Drove up the prices. That was a while ago, though."

"Then we go there," said Tom. "See if Claypool can point us in the right direction."

"Provided he's alive," said Shannon. "I have my doubts about that. If he did summon Gutsy—I doubt Gutsy was in a good mood when he arrived."

"Either way," said Tom. "If we find out where Gutsy came from, maybe—maybe we can send him back."

21

They went to the warehouse district later that day, after the safe had been picked up. The sun was setting as they pulled off the interstate. Shannon drove, a little safer than she had the night before.

"I had never heard of this guy," said Tom. "Apparently he's a big deal on the art scene."

"Eh," said Shannon. "He was for a hot second. He made a big splash with a weird art installation about this alternate universe Sesame Street. It went viral, got popular for a while. He made some other stuff, wasn't as popular."

"How do you know that? Do you follow art stuff?"

"I studied art in college, Tom," said Shannon. "So, yes, I follow 'art stuff'."

"I—I didn't realize," said Tom.

"Some of his stuff was interesting. The Sesame Street was popular, but kind of shallow. Striking visually, which is usually what the general public seizes on, but not much behind it. But some of the other things I saw had something to them. A lot of it said something. Most of it said nothing. But that's a lot of artists. He was fine."

"Well, I can see why they'd have him design Gutsy," said Tom. "If he's famous for the Sesame Street thing."

"Yeah," said Shannon. "I would have just called The Henson Company, but what do I know."

They turned off the surface road, onto Mission Street.

"It's down here somewhere," said Tom. They passed an encampment of homeless people, sitting around a series of burning barrels. And then another. They glanced at them as they passed.

"Thought you said these places were all bought up," said Tom.

"Turns out buying up a lot of cheap land doesn't help house people," said Shannon. "Who would have thought?"

"You might want to lay your sarcasm on a little thicker," said Tom. "I didn't quite get it."

"I'll try harder next time," said Shannon. "We're here."

She turned to the right, and parked in an alley next to a massive warehouse, with a big number 13 stenciled on the corner in white paint.

"I hope it's not locked," said Tom.

"It most certainly is," said Shannon. "Don't worry." She reached behind the seat, pulling out two flashlights, and handing one to Tom. She reached again, and pulled out a crowbar.

"You usually keep that in your car?" asked Tom.

"Yes," said Shannon. "I do, actually. Come on, let's go. The warehouse isn't going to trespass itself."

"Fucking hell," said Tom. He followed her.

"Now to find a way into this place," said Shannon.

"Do you have a lot of experience breaking into warehouses?" asked Tom.

"I studied art in college, Tom," said Shannon. "So, yes. There has to be a single door somewhere. I don't want to open the big double doors unless we have to. Here."

Tom followed the beam of her flashlight to a simple metal door in the wall of the warehouse. It had a handle and a keyhole for a deadbolt. Shannon pulled on it, but it was locked.

"Here, hold my light," said Shannon, handing it over, and then planting a sharp end of the crowbar right underneath the deadbolt. She jammed it in hard, and then leaned on it, flexing it back and forth, between throwing her whole body at it. The door popped with a loud CRACK, the cheap metal sheathing giving way.

"That was easy," said Tom.

"Security is an illusion," said Shannon. She took her flashlight and went inside. Tom followed right behind her.

They walked into the dark warehouse, the dim light from outside barely filtering in.

"What the hell are we looking for?" asked Tom.

"Anything related to Gutsy," said Shannon. "Or Claypool himself. But I don't think he's here."

"Was he living here too?" asked Tom.

"I don't know," said Shannon. "It was the property he owned, so it's a safe bet."

Tom's light danced over the big space, and it suddenly

landed on a streetlight.

"What the fuck?" he asked.

Shannon's light joined him. She revealed a trash can next to the streetlight. Eyes peered out from the trash can.

"Fuck!" yelled Tom. Shannon was silent, walking toward the garbage can. "Jesus, careful, Shannon."

"It's not real, Tom," said Shannon. She stood next to the trash can, and Tom realized this was the alternate Sesame Street set. There was a muppet inside the trash can, or at least a facsimile of one. Not Oscar, though. It was yellow, and didn't have the right number of limbs or eyes.

"Jesus fuck," said Tom. "That's creepy as hell."

"Yeah, in the dark," said Shannon.

Tom's light bounced over the rest of the small recreation of a street. There was a Big Bird creature, big, but pink instead of yellow, and with no face, only a tremendous maw at the end of its long pink neck.

"Gutsy would fit right alongside these guys," said Tom.

"Yeah," said Shannon. "Let's keep moving."

The open space in the middle of the warehouse seemed to contain all of his projects, both complete, and the works in progress. The Sesame Street analogue was front and center, but it wasn't the only one. A lot of the projects seemed to be incomplete to the point of incoherence. Or maybe they were finished, and just incoherent in general.

A splash of red paint on canvas here, with a bucket beneath.

A pile of forks, hundreds, together on the ground. Tom nearly tripped over them.

A sculpture of Tom Brady, but instead of his hands, he had syringes.

What the hell does any of this mean?

"I see what you mean about not saying anything," said Tom, circling the other Tom.

Shannon's voice came from across the room. "I think I see a staircase," she said. "I'm guessing any of the offices are up there."

"I'll be right over," said Tom, turning away from Tom Brady, and he turned with his light, and then Gutsy was there, right in front of him.

"FUCK!" yelled Tom, and he fell backward, his light illuminating the red angry eyes, the mane of crimson hair, he loomed over him, he had followed them, he had followed them—

"Tom?" asked Shannon, and her light was coming over.

"Run, Shannon, run!" he said, scrambling away from Gutsy.

He glanced back, just for a moment, and Gutsy hadn't moved. And then he noticed something wrong, something weird.

That wasn't Gutsy. Not exactly.

The eyes were tilted differently. The hair tufted up off diagonally, instead of straight up. The mane of hair wasn't as thick. His torso was a little slimmer.

Tom stood up, his flashlight on not-Gutsy. Shannon walked up to the impostor. She poked it with the end of the crowbar. It didn't move or say a word.

"That's not Gutsy," said Shannon.

"I realize that now," said Tom. "But it scared the living shit out of me for a second. It's like a prototype Gutsy or something."

"Yeah," said Shannon. "Come on, the stairs are over here.

Unless you want to keep looking at his 'art.'"

"No, I think I'm good," said Tom, with one last look at Notsy.

They moved past all the exhibits to a set of metal stairs in the corner that jangled loudly as they walked up them.

"This place is falling apart," said Tom.

"No, it just feels like it," said Shannon. They walked up the stairs, twenty feet up onto a catwalk that led to a series of offices.

"Anything useful is probably up here," said Shannon. They looked down the catwalk, a series of four doors on the right. "At least it'll make it easy to eliminate anything useless."

"You want me to lead the way?" asked Tom.

"I have the crowbar," said Shannon. "I'm not expecting trouble."

"I just wanted to put the offer out there," said Tom.

Shannon tried the first door. It wasn't locked. It creaked open. She stepped in, with Tom right behind her.

Their lights illuminated the space. It was a relatively undecorated bedroom. A double bed sat in the corner, on a boxspring on the floor, without a frame. A couple of bookshelves stood along the wall, half empty. A lonely chair was there, and next to it, a small dresser. Everything was covered in a layer of dust.

"He lived here, at least," said Shannon. "But it's been a long time since then."

"Onto door number 2," said Tom. "I'll take this one."

He moved onto the next door, identical to the first. He pushed it open, his flashlight leading the way. The first thing it landed on was a toilet.

"Well, I found the bathroom," said Tom. There was a toilet, a sink, and a simple shower stall, but not much else. Shannon peeked inside.

"Can confirm, is a bathroom," said Shannon. "Also not used in a long time."

Shannon moved ahead to the third door. Tom joined right behind her, and she opened it. It was a storage closet, filled to the brim with boxes.

"Three strikes," said Shannon.

"We can call this one a foul tip," said Tom. "There might be something useful inside the boxes, but we can come back to them."

"The last door is yours," said Shannon. "Hope that we don't strike out."

Tom pushed it open, and was immediately assaulted by a terrible stink.

"Ugh," said Tom, pushing the door open, but covering his nose with his other hand. "Something stinks." He walked in, his flashlight scanning the room. Shannon was right behind him.

This room was filled. On one wall was a desk, a standing desk, with three different monitors, and a giant touch sensitive screen alongside. The desk was covered in notebooks, and sketches were hung up alongside each of the monitors. There was a single bookcase nearby, and then another table, covered in electronic equipment.

"What's that?" asked Shannon. Her light was focused on a massive device in the center of the room, a huge machine, covered in gears, and tubes, and other things Tom couldn't identify, not without closer examination.

"I don't know," said Tom. "What the fuck is that smell

coming from—" and then his flashlight landed on the cause, lying in the corner. His beam spotted bones, stripped of flesh. Long dried blood. Pieces of meat, mostly rotted, but still putrid.

"Claypool," said Shannon.

22

"Jesus," said Tom. "He's been dead a long time."

"I'm willing to guess it was Gutsy," said Shannon.

"Probably a safe assumption," said Tom. "Fucking hell. He brought him here." Tom pointed his flashlight over to the mysterious machine in the middle of the room. "My next guess, which might be a slightly riskier one, is with that thing."

"Don't touch it," said Shannon.

"I wasn't planning on it," said Tom. "At least not yet."

Shannon scanned the room again, and then walked to the wall and flipped on a switch. The fluorescents on the ceiling blinked on, lighting the room brightly.

"Hey, power," said Tom. "It's nice to see things." He glanced at the remains in the corner. "Well, maybe not."

"Jesus," said Shannon. "What a mess. What did he do?"

"He brought Gutsy here," said Tom. "Look at this." He pointed at the machine. It was much more involved than it first looked, now that they could get a good look at it. What the hell—

"I've never seen anything like it," said Shannon. "There are tubes of some liquid attached to it."

"Yeah," said Tom. "It looks like—yeah, they used to hold blood." The tubes were stuck into something that vaguely resembled a car engine, or at least what Tom thought of when he imagined a car engine. There were belts, and gears, but there were also the empty ampules that once contained blood, still stained vaguely red. Cords and wires ran from a power supply that was attached to it. A small aperture rose from the top of the machine, and it pointed at a pad in the far center of the room, a target on the ground.

"What the fuck is this thing?" asked Shannon.

"Let's look in his computer," said Tom. "Maybe there are answers in there."

Shannon walked over to it, and tentatively pushed the power button on the tower unit, standing underneath the desk. It whirred on.

"Well, step number one was a success," she said. The main monitor ran through the boot process, and then asked for a login. "Fuck. It could be anything."

"Wait a second," said Tom. He looked closer at the screen. "It's not asking for a login. It's asking for a fingerprint ID." Tom looked over the desk. There was a small box next to the mouse, with a glass top. He pointed at it.

"Oh, Jesus," said Shannon. "How are we going—" Tom looked at her, and then looked over at the body.

"Maybe Gutsy left us the right finger," said Tom.

"Fuck," said Shannon.

"I'll get it, if you—"

"No," said Shannon. "I can do it." She walked over to the remains of Claypool, looking over the scattered bits of meat. She buried her mouth and nose in the crook of her elbow, and then bent down and grabbed something from the floor. Shannon held it between thumb and forefinger. "I hope this is it."

"Do the honors," said Tom.

Shannon placed the pad of the finger on the little black box, and the system started, and Shannon gingerly placed the finger down on the ground, away.

"I don't want to lose it," said Shannon with a grimace.

"What are we looking for?" asked Tom. He scanned the monitor. The man's desktop was a mess. It was covered in icons and files. Some of them were named specifically. There seemed to be a dozen different iterations of files named after Gutsy.

Gutsy design.png

Gutsy design final.png

Gutsy design final final.png

But others were named vague nonsense like "today's work.docx" or "thoughts.jpg".

Shannon wasn't looking at the screen at all. She was flipping through the notebooks that were on the desk, piled up high.

"Most of these are just design ideas, for art in general," said Shannon. "Just sketches. Maybe worth a deeper look later, if we come up empty." She picked up another. "This is all just Gutsy sketches." She showed Tom a few different pages, and they were all just alternate designs for Gutsy, still recognizable, if a little weird. To be fair, Gutsy's final design was weird as well.

Shannon picked up a final notebook.

"This one's empty," said Shannon. "Well, I can relate to that. I collect empty notebooks."

Tom looked back at the monitor. He clicked and dragged icons around, sorting them into different piles. One pile was probably useless, another was anything with potential, and another were the strongest files, the ones with almost definite answers.

There had been none for that pile yet, most of them heading straight to the garbage, filled with memes, and drawing references, and selfies with what looked like a girlfriend.

"Hope she made it out okay," said Tom.

"Well, her body isn't here," said Shannon. "There's that, at least."

"Wait, this might be something," said Tom. There was a folder on the desktop, labeled "vlogs". He double-clicked. "Jackpot." There were several dozen files, long video recordings of himself. He opened the first file. The file opened, and Tom maximized it.

Norman Claypool filled the screen, standing in front of this desk, staring into what looked like the webcam that was still attached to the computer. Claypool was thin, wearing all black, with a bald head. His dark eyes stared into the camera.

"Hi, guys, Claypool here. I'm starting up this vlog series to give you guy's an inside look at what I'm working on, on all aspects of my life, and an up-close sneak peek on all my art. And I wanted to start this series off with a bang. Something new, something really exciting that I've been researching." He held up a book.

"What the hell?" asked Tom.

"I've been digging for several years for this. Contacting every one I could in the art world, and a huge variety of booksellers, all over the world. It took some time, and pretty big investment, but honestly, it was all worth it, now that I hold it in my hands. Now you're probably wondering—what book is it, Claypool?"

"Get on with it," said Shannon.

"He was going to put this all on Youtube," said Tom.

"Not anymore he isn't," said Shannon.

"This book is titled 'Mechanical Means of Interplanar Communication' by John Dawkins. Crazy, huh? You've probably never heard of this, and for good reason. Mr. Dawkins died years and years ago, alone on his isolated farmland in Kansas. Only a few dozen copies of this book exist, almost all of them hand bound by Dawkins himself."

"Fuck me," said Tom, staring over at Shannon, and then at the big machine in the middle of the room.

"Dawkins claimed he could communicate with other planes of existence through intricate machines, properly tuned. This book contains the means to build those machines, and instructions on how to use them. Now—I don't want to get ahead of myself. I don't believe this will actually work. But I do want to document my journey as I build one of these machines, and operate it for the first time. Exciting, right? And I want you to come along for the ride—"

Tom closed the video.

"There's dozens of these things," said Tom. Shannon was already typing on her phone.

"Nothing from him on Youtube," said Shannon.

"He never published them," said Tom. "I wonder why. I guess I get it. He's an artist. Wanted to build this strange machine out of this weird old book. Get himself some publicity."

"Unfortunately, the weird old machine worked," said Shannon.

"Well, I don't know if it worked," said Tom. "We don't know if it was *supposed* to bring Gutsy here."

"It did something," said Shannon. "And ended up costing Claypool."

Tom skipped ahead a few videos and hit play. Claypool was using a different camera, and Tom looked over to see what he guessed was it sitting on the table near them.

Claypool sat on a stool, the book on the table. A few parts had been assembled, and he held another one, but he looked confused.

"You'll have to pardon my confusion, guys. I've had all these machined by my friend Gary, but this part doesn't seem to have a home." He stared at the part, a long metal cylinder. "What the hell is this supposed—"

Tom closed the video.

"Some of these are hours long," said Tom. "No one wants to watch hours of a dude struggling to put together a machine."

"Some people put on videos to fall asleep to," said Shannon.

"Fair enough," said Tom. He jumped ahead again.

Claypool stared at the camera. His eyes looked haggard now, and there were bags building underneath them.

"I'm almost complete with the machine itself," said Claypool. "It is surely the hardest part of this project, assembling the device. Dawkins' instructions are difficult to interpret, compounded by the fact that some instructions are in code, which I've had to break, multiple times." Claypool looked back at the machine, which looked to be 90% the size of the machine that sat behind Tom and Shannon.

He looked back at the camera. "But that only adds to the intrigue. Why would Dawkins make his own instructions that much more difficult to use? Another mystery, one I can answer—"

Tom closed it.

"We're getting closer, at least," said Tom. He skipped ahead even more. The second video from the end.

Claypool was on camera again. He looked even more haggard, his beard growing out in rough patches. His eyes were scattershot, looking at the camera, and then not, bouncing around.

"It's ready," he said. "Only the small finishing touches, and then it'll be ready for its first full operation. But I must test it first." He moved over to the machine, which looked much like it did now, in the present day.

"Dawkins' book is incomplete. But after my trials and tribulations, I've realized that it is incomplete on purpose. He wanted me to fill in the gaps, fill in the details. It was a test, a test that I passed with flying colors. The proof lies in front of me." He gestured toward the different parts of the machine. "This is the power. I patched in a higher power supply, to compensate for the different loads we're able to achieve nowadays. I hope the electrical system here can take it. Now, to test, to see if it'll turn on." He cautiously pushed the red rubber button, and the machine began to churn, starting up, gears moving. The lights flickered for a moment, but then stayed on. The machine churned for a few moments, and Claypool watched closely, and then, satisfied, pushed the button once again. The machine spun down.

"Success," he said, smiling wide. Tom noticed one of his teeth was missing. "But the machine is not complete. It will require one more thing to run. One more thing to fuel it. My blood. I will draw it tonight, after I turn off the camera. Tomorrow, it helps power impossibility."

The video ended.

"Well, he got the machine working," said Tom.

"Still doesn't answer why the hell he ended up summoning Gutsy," said Shannon.

"I don't think he intended to," said Tom. "At this point, I don't think he was all there. Building the machine, getting it working—I think he was obsessed to the point of madness. You ready for the last video?"

"As ready as I'll ever be," said Shannon. Tom double-clicked.

"The day is here," said Claypool, to the camera. He stood in front of the machine. "I've inserted my blood into the device, providing the final fuel. The only thing remaining is to dial in a direction for my signal. To decide who I want to communicate with. With this, Dawkins' provided no documentation at all. There are three dials, each of them numbered differently. One is 1-10, one is 1-100, and the third is letterered, from A to Z." Claypool shook his head. "This was one of the most difficult choices, about where to direct the machine. But I paid an exorbitant price for what I was told was one of Dawkins' own notebooks." He pulled it onto the camera. "There is writing all over it, much indecipherable. But scribbled on one of the final pages is 6, 99, X. That is as good a starting place as any." He walked over to the machine. "All that is left is to start the device. I will be the first to record contact with an interplanar being." Claypool pushed the red button, and the machine spun up, much like in the previous video. But this time it did more. It vibrated, shaking hard, and pieces of ceiling fell on the video. "Oh my, it's working! It's working!" yelled Claypool.

The aperture on the device glowed, a hard, bright light, ranging through a rainbow of colors, before finally settling on red. A familiar shade of red. A beam of light emerged from the aperture, the same red color, and settled on the pad on the ground. The red light filled the room, covering everything.

The machine vibrated harder and faster, almost disappearing into a blur, and in one moment the pad that was empty was now full. It was now occupied by Gutsy. A blue smoke rose from the machine.

He stood there, still.

"What?" yelled Claypool, staring at Gutsy. "What is this? This was supposed to—"

Gutsy turned to face him. A sound emerged from him, a terrible gnashing sound that hurt Tom's ears. Shannon covered hers reflexively in response.

"Why are you here?" asked Claypool. "Why—"

And that was the last sound Claypool uttered that wasn't a scream, as Gutsy moved to him and attacked, ripping him limb from limb. Tom looked away. He looked back when the screams had stopped, as well as the terrible noises of Gutsy guzzling down parts of Norman.

Gutsy was there for a moment, and then he was gone.

23

The video continued for a few moments longer, and then the power cut out, and the video ended a second later.

"Must have overloaded the circuit or something," said Shannon. Tom took a deep breath, and looked at the device.

"Why Gutsy, though?" asked Tom. "That's the thing I still don't understand."

"Look around," said Shannon. "There's designs for him everywhere. Claypool was definitely still working, even as he was building the machine. There's even that prototype downstairs."

"And?" asked Tom. "Gutsy is some kind of interplanar predator. He doesn't look like Gutsy."

"You said it yourself, when you saw him on the other world. He looked like something else," said Shannon. "But how has he hunted, here? He hides. He stays invisible, un-seen, strikes at his target, kills them, eats them, and then disappears again. Sure, he's strong, but he wants to blend in, for now, at least."

"So, he's a chameleon," said Tom. "He found himself in a new place, scanned his environment, and became Gutsy."

"Yes," said Shannon. "It makes the most sense. Even Claypool didn't expect it."

"Claypool was surprised he summoned anything at all," said Tom. "By the end there, he seemed like he expected it to work."

"The book was called communication," said Shannon. "Not transportation."

"Claypool said he made alterations to the machine," said Tom. "Maybe he made it into a transportation device, ac-cidentally." Tom paused. "Wait a second—how did Gutsy know how to get to the arena?"

"Instinct, maybe," said Shannon. "He needed a new home."

"I guess," said Tom. He stared at the machinery. "Does it have a reverse button?"

"I don't see one," said Shannon, moving around the en-gine. "Only button is the red power button. The dials. The vials that hold the blood."

Tom looked over the bookshelf. Dawkins' book was right there, on the end, and he grabbed it. It felt flimsy. To be fair, it was old, had been hand bound, and Claypool had probably abused the hell out of it.

He flipped it open.

"Be careful," said Shannon.

"It's a book, Shannon," said Tom. "It's not a magic spell.

It's not the Necronomicon."

"I'm just nervous," said Shannon. "God, it stinks in here."

"Well, as soon as we can get out, we can," said Tom. "We have to figure this out first."

He looked over the book, scanning the pages. The typeset was easy to read, but man, it was hard to follow. Dawkins' writing jumped over itself, constantly referring to other parts of the book. It was a technical manual written like a novel, and he understood now why Claypool had so much trouble with it. How the hell could you follow this? You needed to take a class on this thing to understand it.

"Dawkins was a terrible writer," said Tom. He continued to scan the pages. "And he seemed absolutely insane, on top of it. Those dials aren't random. He seemed to think that there were that many permutations of planes out there, and that you could reach any of them using this machine."

"One was enough," said Shannon. "I don't care about thousands of worlds. We need to know how to send Gutsy back."

"It would take me days to read through this," said Tom. "And even then, I don't think I'd understand it. Hell, the timestamps on these videos—" Tom scanned them quickly. "—it took Claypool over a year to build the machine."

"We don't have a year," said Shannon. "There's two of him now. Two of him, to feed twice as much. If he keeps multiplying—"

"It'll be exponential," said Tom, and the vision he saw flew through his mind. "You're right. What about Dawkins' notebook, where Claypool found the destination code? Maybe it's in there."

Shannon flipped through it. "It's all nonsense. Here.

'Communication is key. If I am to be an emissary, I must first negotiate terms. There will be a language barrier. I will be the universal Rosetta Stone." Shannon stared at Tom. "There's so much. 'Fire is a universal deterrent. It transcends interplanar barriers.' What the fuck does that mean?"

"Wait, that might be useful," said Tom. "Does that mean Gutsy is weak to fire?"

"We burnt him up," said Shannon. "It didn't stop him."

"No, that's not true," said Tom. "We burnt up the suit. Maybe when he's awake, it does more damage. It's worth a shot. Maybe it'll slow him down."

"Claypool studied this stuff for a long time. He had to take notes. Look on his computer."

Tom put the book aside, and went back to the PC. "It's a complete mess," said Tom. "There are icons everywhere, and I can't figure out his organizational system at all—"

"What are you talking about?" asked Shannon.

"Folders, with clear and concise names? And then files in those folders? And then, if necessary, you repeat that?"

"Why the hell do you think there's a search function?" asked Shannon. "Why should I click through a dozen sub-folders when I can just search for what I want—"

Tom stared at her. "You do that?"

"Yes," said Shannon. "It's much faster—"

"But at what cost?"

"Jesus," said Shannon. She moved to the keyboard, went to search, and typed in "reverse".

"There's no way that'll work," said Tom. "Do you think he just seeded all his notes with keywords—"

"It's right here."

"What? Really?"

"I think so," said Shannon. She double clicked into the file. It was a long text file, which started organized and quickly devolved into randomness. Shannon searched again for "reverse" and clicked through her findings.

"Here," she said. "The aperture can be reversed. The stream can go both ways. I haven't tested this, but Dawkins mentioned this specifically. Why?"

"Because Dawkins knew something could come through," said Tom. "And he might want to send it back."

"We should look into that Dawkins guy," said Shannon.

"I'm guessing he's long dead," said Tom. "And we don't have time."

"You're right," said Shannon.

Tom walked over to the machinery. There was a small piece of glass or crystal at the front of the machine, the place where the light emerged in Claypool's video.

"Is that the aperture?" asked Shannon.

"Yeah, I think so," said Tom. He reached out a finger to touch it.

"Careful."

"It's not even on, Shannon," said Tom. He touched it. It remained in place. Then he saw the small catch below it, and he disengaged it, a small piece of metal now hanging. He touched the piece of crystal again, and it swiveled now. Tom reversed it, the convex side now facing out. He reengaged the metal catch, and now the aperture again was stuck in place.

"That's it?" asked Shannon. "That was easy."

"Well, it hasn't done anything yet," said Tom. "Do you think we can move it?"

"We'll have to," said Shannon. "I doubt we can lure Gutsy

here."

"Where should we move it?" asked Tom.

"The arena," said Shannon. "Where else? We hit him at home. Hell, maybe we can just stack the suit on the pad, and hit the button."

"Suits," said Tom.

"Jesus, don't remind me," said Shannon. "How much does it weigh?"

Tom went to the side of the machine and lifted at an edge. "Fuck. It's heavy. But we can do it together. Just have to be careful. Don't think there are replacement parts for this thing."

"There might be, honestly," said Shannon. "If we dig through those boxes."

"I hope it doesn't come to that," said Tom. He traced the various cords with his eyes. "There really isn't that many. No worse than a computer. It'll mostly be remembering where everything plugs in."

"Take pictures with your phone," said Shannon. "Of everything. I'm going to pull my car into the warehouse, see if I can get the lights turned on downstairs. It'll be way easier to load everything up that way."

"Right now?" asked Tom.

"What are we waiting for? More dead bodies?" asked Shannon. She left the room. Tom heard her walk down the catwalk and down the stairs, the metal reverberating.

He took out his phone and took pictures of everything involving the machine. Every connection, wire, and cord. They would have to unplug all of this stuff before they moved it, and plug it in later. Jesus, this would be a nightmare. But hey, if it stopped Gutsy, it was all worth it. Cloudy would be the last victim, and they could move on with their lives.

Tom took pictures from every angle, but then his finger slipped, and he accidentally switched to the selfie camera, and—

And Gutsy stood behind him.

The second suit.

Tom turned to run but Gutsy's red hands snatched him, one wrapping itself around his neck, and beginning to squeeze. He struggled, as hard as he could, but Gutsy was too strong for him.

Gutsy's other hand went to his stomach.

Oh God, no, he's going to rip me apart.

Tom felt it pushing into him, and he tried to scream, but there was no breath, he was going to die here, God damn it, going to die in some warehouse, killed by a hockey mascot.

"I got the lights on downstairs, the car is pulled inside, and—" Shannon stopped, seeing Gutsy in front of her. Gutsy paused to stare at her, and then she disappeared, running out the door.

What the fuck, Shannon

But within ten seconds, she was back, bursting through the door and charging at Gutsy.

What the hell are you doing?

But then he saw. Shannon held up an aerosol can, and sprayed it at Gutsy, and then held up a lighter, and flicked it once, twice, and it ignited, and the spray burst into flame. The flame caught Gutsy in the arm and he ignited, his whole arm on fire. Gutsy screamed in pain, a terrible noise that Tom couldn't classify, a noise from somewhere else, high pitched, almost inaudible.

Gutsy dropped him, and he could breath, and his hand went to his stomach, and it came back wet with blood, but it was only a surface wound, it hadn't gone too deep.

"Turn the machine on!" yelled Shannon. She still blasted Gutsy with the flaming aerosol, a gout of flame spraying toward the creature. He backed away, something Tom had never seen him do.

The fire does work.

"I—" started Tom, looking at the machinery. The big red button stared at him. "It needs blood to work!"

"You have blood!" yelled Shannon back. She had cornered Gutsy on the pad, and did her best to corral him. "Hurry!"

Tom looked to the ampules, and popped them off, one by one, scooping the blood that leaked from his stomach into them, as fast as he could. He hoped it was enough, popping them back into place.

"Hurry!"

"Get away from the pad!" yelled Tom as he pushed the button. The machine turned on, just like in the video, churning, pumping, and then vibrating as it picked up speed. The blood got sucked inside, and the same red light glowed out of the aperture. Gutsy stood on the pad, his body moving, breaking itself down, trying desperately to put out the fire. Tom saw where the fire had hurt him, had slowed him down.

Then the fire was out, and Gutsy stared at them, but the machine vibrated still, and then the red light engulfed Gutsy, and Tom closed his eyes, his hands up, and then the device kicked off, and Tom opened his eyes, and Gutsy was gone.

They were alone again with Claypool's corpse.

"Well, at least we know it works," said Shannon.

24

The other Gutsy suit was gone when they got back to the arena.

"Where is he?" asked Shannon.

"I don't know," said Tom. "Do you think he knows about the machine?"

"He knows he got here somehow," said Shannon. "—wait, do you think he and the copy, like, share a hive mind, or something?"

"Well, I hadn't until now," said Tom. "But I sure hope not. He's probably out hunting, building up strength, with the second suit sent to get us. Probably thought we wouldn't be any trouble. Let's unload the machine and plug it in."

"No, not yet," said Shannon.

"What do you mean, not yet?" asked Tom.

"Come with me," said Shannon. "We shouldn't go any-where alone. We stick together. Much easier to handle Gutsy when there's two of us."

"Yeah, when one of us has something flammable, may-be."

"You're just lucky that Claypool had hairspray," said Shannon. "But that's what we need, before we set up the ma-chine." She walked off, toward the utility area of the arena. Tom followed. His stomach ached from where Gutsy had hurt him. They had grabbed a spare shirt from Claypool's dresser and tied it around his stomach. It would do for now.

"Where are we going?" asked Tom. Shannon went down the hallway, made a left, and then another left, through a utility door.

Skates always leaves it open," said Shannon. "He hates the electronic locks."

"What if it had been locked?"

"I would have broken in," said Shannon. "We're well past that."

"I guess you're right," said Tom. "What are we looking for?"

"This," said Shannon, and she picked it up.

"Is that a—"

"Yep," said Shannon, smiling. "Flamethrower. To melt the ice, in a pinch. But instead, we'll melt a Gutsy."

"I hope it doesn't come to that," said Tom.

"I'd rather have it and not need it, then need it and not have it," said Shannon. "Skates showed me how to use it. Light the pilot light, open the gas, and pull the trigger."

They returned to "their" area of the arena. They carried the core of the machine in, Tom struggling with his end, his stomach straining at the weight.

"You gonna make it?" asked Shannon.

"Yeah, I'll make it," said Tom. "Hurts like hell, but it beats getting my guts slurped."

"You do have a way with words," said Shannon. They set down the machine on the ground, and then came back with the various wires, cords, and plugs that went into it. Tom pulled up the pictures on his phone, and started inserting them all back where they belonged. After twenty minutes of tracing snaking wires, everything was plugged in like it was supposed to be. Shannon plopped down the mat right where the aperture aimed.

Tom then realized the silence.

"Where the hell is everyone?" he asked.

"It's 2 AM," said Shannon.

"Yeah, but someone from security should have seen us by now, and wondered what the hell we're doing. No one. Not a peep."

"Do you really want people asking us questions right now?" asked Shannon. "We don't have any logical explanations for this. The safe made a certain kind of sense. This? This is Ghostbusters."

"No, I don't want questions, but I also don't want more people dead," said Tom.

"They're fine," said Shannon. "Gutsy doesn't feed here."

"Not yet," said Tom. "Well, everything is set up. We just need to give it blood."

"I'll do it this time," said Shannon.

"You sure?" asked Tom. "I've already—"

Shannon had popped each of the ampules off the machine, and held them in her hand. She grabbed a box cutter from a nearby pallet.

"I would clean—" started Tom, but Shannon had already nicked her finger with the sharp edge of the blade, and held it over each ampule, until they were filled with blood. She popped the ampules back onto the machine, and pocketed the box cutter, and then slid her finger into her mouth.

"I'll be fine," said Shannon. "It's ready to go, now. We just need Gutsy."

"It's only a matter of time," said Tom. "He always comes back."

"I don't want to just wait here," said Shannon. "I want to—"

A remote scream echoed down the halls in the bowels of the arena.

"You were saying?" asked Tom.

"We have the flamethrower," said Shannon.

"We have to get him."

"So be it."

Shannon grabbed the weapon, and they moved toward the scream. It had been distant. And with the way sound traveled in these hallways, it was difficult to tell where it came from.

Shannon led the way, the pilot light lit on the flame-thrower, the fuel canister open. One quick pull of the trigger, and it would belch fire.

They prowled through the halls, listening for more screams, looking for any sign of trouble.

Then they saw the first sign of blood.

"Well, we know where security is," said Tom.

"I—I don't know who that is," said Shannon.

The body had been destroyed, ripped apart, and consumed, just like all the others. Tom knew multiple members of the security staff by name, but like Shannon had said, this person was unidentifiable.

"Oh god," said Shannon, looking down the hallway. A trail of blood lay ahead of them, and it led to another body.

"It was Sherry," said Shannon, looking away, forcing back tears. Sherry was the only woman on the security team. Aside from that, there was little left identifying her. Gutsy had destroyed her, pulled out her organs, and left her body empty. Tom looked away. Even after all the carnage he had witnessed, he still had his limits.

"He doesn't feed here," said Tom. "He doesn't want to be found." Facts they thought they knew about Gutsy. Facts they were wrong about.

"Look at this," said Shannon. "He was angry. More than angry. Enraged. He wanted to take it out on whoever was closest. That meant the security staff. Maintenance. Anyone working here."

"He lost his twin," said Tom. "He must have felt him die. He wanted to take it out on someone. On some people."

"Senseless," said Shannon.

"Not senseless," said Tom. "Making him stronger. So he can make more of himself again. We have to move quickly. If he makes a double, we don't have a chance. We can't fight two of him at once."

They followed farther, chasing the gore.

"He killed them all," said Tom, as they passed two more bodies. "There's no way to hide from this. They'll know it was someone here."

"I think Gutsy is past hiding," said Shannon. "We don't even know if he even has to stay in this form."

"Where is he?" asked Tom. "Gutsy!" His yell echoed down the hallway.

"What are you doing?" asked Shannon.

"I'm done running from this son of a bitch," said Tom. "I'm tired of him killing. I'm tired of him *feeding*."

"Gutsy!" Tom yelled again, moving down the hallway. Blood still trailed, but Tom wasn't looking at the bodies anymore. His eyes were up, searching for a big red body. They would burn him to nothing, drag him to the machine, and send him back to Hell. He was tired of feeling weak. He was tired of feeling powerless. Shannon walked with him, the flamethrower ready. Her eyes scanned every shadow.

"You can't hide from us, Gutsy!" yelled Tom. "Maybe you can slink in the shadows, and attack from behind like a coward, but not us! Not us!"

There was no answer, and they had almost reached the end of the arena's depths.

"How are we going to get him to the machine?" asked Shannon.

"We'll roast him, and drag him back," said Tom. "We end it now."

They still couldn't find him, and they turned a corner, and they faced a long, twenty foot wide hallway, the only place left on this side of the arena.

Pools of blood dotted the concrete, laying a trail to the end of the space.

"There's not much over here," said Shannon. "Mostly just storage space, with some machinery. No one works over here, as far as I know."

There were no more screams or shouts. Only silence.

"He's down there," said Tom.

"It's a trap, Tom," said Shannon. "If it wasn't obvious before, it certainly is now. He wants us down there. We already sent half of him back to wherever he came from."

"And we're going to finish the job," said Tom. "He doesn't know you have that. I'll go in front, and then you can surprise him. Alright?"

Shannon eyed him for a long second and then nodded, falling behind him. Tom went ahead, doing his best to avoid stepping in the blood. There was so, so much of it. He'd never seen so much, never in his life. Tom didn't think there was that much blood in a person.

They slowly crept down the hallway. Tom paused before each intersecting doorway, peeking to see if they were open, if any of the blood led inside. But none of them did. The blood led only to the end of the hallway.

They advanced, and soon, they were near the end. There was one more door on the left. Tom peeked around the edge, and saw it was open. The trail of blood led right to it.

Tom glanced at Shannon, who trailed behind him roughly twenty feet. He motioned to the door, and she nodded back, holding the flamethrower, ready to use it.

Tom crept around the corner, to the open door, hiding along the edge. The blood was thicker here. It wasn't possible. How could one person have this much blood?

He would have to step in it. There was no avoiding it now. He stepped, staining his shoes. He listened from the outside of the door.

A wet dripping is all he heard, the noise of splattering liquid.

He didn't want to look, he didn't want to see what caused the noise, his heart cold, his guts aching. But Gutsy had to pay. They would send him back.

Tom stepped out, and through the open door. He didn't look back, trusting Shannon would be behind him, covering him, ready.

He stepped through, his feet in the blood, and saw the source of the noise.

Gutsy stood there, in the storage room. He wasn't alone.

Tom remembered now, talking to Skates, shortly after he was hired. Skates mentioned his own break room. Where he would go to unwind after working a long game day. Skates had never told him where it was.

Well, this was clearly it.

Gutsy stood in the middle of the room, holding a corpse by the ankle, above his head, almost touching the ceiling. The corpse dripped blood from its throat, torn open by Gutsy.

Tom recognized the body.

It was Skates.

Gutsy stared at him. He had been waiting. He opened his maw, the terrible void, the well of blood and chaos. Gutsy opened his mouth wide, wider than possible, unhinged his jaw, and swallowed Skates whole.

25

Skates was gone, in an instant.

"You fucker!" yelled Tom, and he charged, knowing it was the worst thing he could do. Gutsy didn't move, only waited and stared as Tom ran at him, his unhinged jaw closing shut, Skates' body now a part of Gutsy.

Tom charged across the impossible pool of blood and then he slid, and Gutsy grabbed him by the throat, and lifted him in the air, and tossed him backward, back through the open door. Tom landed hard on the concrete floor, and he felt a crack in his side, and every breath hurt. He was covered in blood now, his body wet and aching. Before he could move, Gutsy was on top of him, and pulled him up, and threw him again.

You could have stood aside. This was not necessary.

Tom slammed into the far wall, and his ribs screamed in pain. He forced a breath in through anguished lungs. Gutsy could have ripped him apart in a moment, but he wanted Tom to suffer.

"Burn, you fucker," said Shannon, as she unleashed a gout of flame at Gutsy. The heat in the enclosed hallway was incredible. Shannon had turned the release valve as wide as it got, and the flamethrower released a massive firestorm which engulfed Gutsy.

A noise came from Gutsy, a terrible wet scream, an unholy piercing impossible cacophony, that ripped through Tom's ears and mind. It was an awful sound, unearthly, but a part of Tom enjoyed nonetheless, even as his body recoiled.

It meant they had hurt Gutsy.

Gutsy floundered on his feet, the flames engulfing him, lighting his malleable, alien flesh on fire. He danced, trying to morph his way away from the fire, and Tom saw the chameleon beneath. Gutsy's skin was on fire, the red fur melting away, and Gutsy would do anything to get away from the flames.

But Shannon didn't stop firing. Tom pushed back against the wall, and slid his way around, away from the heat as much as he could, back to the other side of Shannon.

Shannon advanced on Gutsy, getting closer and closer, making sure the fire destroyed him. They would burn him until he was incapacitated, and then drag his body to the machine and send him back.

The fireball was huge, and the flames wicked away at Gutsy's flesh. And it was flesh now, plain to see. Hidden behind the facade of the mascot costume, shifting muscle and fat could be seen, sinew and skin, only adopting the appearance of Gutsy. And Gutsy's skin still shifted, undulating, moving in waves, as the blaze battered and roasted him.

Shannon didn't let up, her face determined, tears in her eyes. As Gutsy burned, Tom let hope into his heart again. They would beat this thing, finally. The bloodshed would end. They would win.

Shannon continued to burn it, and more and more of Gutsy was on fire, unable to avoid the inferno.

Just another minute or so, and this would be over.

But then Tom saw something from Gutsy, something his mind couldn't wrap itself around. Not at first. But as he watched, he understood.

Gutsy's flesh was moving, trying to avoid the fire, each piece of the creature doing its best to ward off the flames. But Tom hadn't been focusing on the big picture, on the plan Gutsy had.

How could Gutsy have a plan? He was on fire.

They had surprised Gutsy with the flamethrower, assuredly, but the creature had crossed dimensions, and had overtaken worlds, and they had already burned the other Gutsy.

It had learned.

Gutsy wasn't roiling away from the flames without control. He had been shedding his skin, pulling away flesh from himself. Anything that ignited, he would push away, slowly removing it.

But not only that, not only removing the destroyed flesh, the danger of the burning fuel.

No. He was using it as a shield.

And as Tom watched, as Shannon fired the flamethrower, the shield of flesh was completely off Gutsy, and it moved in front, obscuring him from their views, only the burning piece of Gutsy visible, and then Gutsy was behind Shannon, and with incredible speed, the flamethrower was crushed, one massive paw of Gutsy crushing the fuel lines, and throwing Shannon aside, slamming into the wall. Only the canisters on her back kept her alive, absorbing most of the blow.

Shannon laid dazed against the wall, blinking, trying to regain her senses. Gutsy stood there, looking the same, despite the loss of flesh, and then walked over to the skin shield, and grabbed the burning flesh, and sluiced it through the drying pools of blood, and the fire squelched out.

With the fire gone, Gutsy reabsorbed the flesh, disappearing into its being, and Tom was frozen, all hope extinguished.

I AM BEYOND YOU.

The low sinister tone was gone now, Gutsy bellowing its thoughts at him, and Tom recoiled, and then Gutsy was there, holding him by the throat. Tom couldn't breathe, and he beat at the arms of Gutsy, but it did nothing. He hit him as hard as he could, but it didn't matter.

Even at diminished strength, you cannot harm me. You are nothing. You are food. Do you think your tricks will stop me? I have harvested a dozen worlds, and I will harvest dozens more. I am spread. I am reach. I am everything, in the past and future. There is no world that I will not touch.

Tom was filled with Gutsy's horrible voice, and he tried to yell for help, and he looked to Shannon. She had dumped the flamethrower, and ran down the hall, back to where they came from, and Tom's heart ached. She had abandoned him.

It was for the best. They both shouldn't die, not here.

Maybe she could still stop Gutsy. Tom would pay for their mistakes.

How much life is in you? How long can you last without air?

Tom struggled. He wouldn't go without a fight. But what fight he had was waning. His lungs screamed in pain, and he felt darkness enter his mind. His arms beat weakly at Gutsy, but they did nothing.

Do not worry. You will join your brethren inside me. You will join the void that feeds.

And then Tom heard a noise. A groaning noise.

The sound of an engine.

Tom forced his eyes open, with what little energy he had, and then he saw it.

Shannon hadn't run away. She'd gone for another weapon.

Gutsy stared at Tom, either not hearing Shannon, or not caring.

It would cost him.

The zamboni hit Gutsy at full speed. Zambonis don't go fast, but they're big, and heavy, and it plowed over Gutsy. Gutsy dropped Tom and he fell to the side, ragged breath coming back into his lungs, the stars in his vision disappearing. There was a terrible thunk as the zamboni ran over Gutsy, bouncing up and down.

But the true damage wasn't done by the weight of the machine, but by the blade at the back.

Skates had taken the time to show Tom the zamboni one day. Tom didn't know what it was, only that they drove it between periods. Just looked like a big block on wheels.

"It resurfaces the ice, Tommy," Skates had said. "It can

spray water, you know, to help make the ice stronger. But, it also has a big blade on the back. Super sharp. Dangerous as hell. Stay away from that thing."

Tom couldn't see what the blade did to Gutsy, not at first, but he could hear it, as the razor sharp blade, lowered as far as it could go, sliced through Gutsy. Gutsy screamed again, louder, a noise that Tom had never heard before, not in his life. The zamboni tumbled off him, and Gutsy laid on the concrete, sliced into ribbons, floundering. Awful noises came from the creature, and it reached out for Tom, and Tom scooted backwards, away from its hands.

Gutsy wasn't invincible, and they'd hurt it again. But it was already healing, piecing itself back together.

But then Shannon wheeled the zamboni around and ran over him again.

It thumped and bounced over him, the zamboni not meant for that, and Tom worried it would stall, but the machine was tough, and the blades at the back of it chewed through Gutsy one more time, and crimson pieces of moving flesh flew out from the side of the thing, all of them desperately searching for purchase, to find each other once again, to become one again.

But there was one difference. Some of the pieces stopped moving altogether. Gutsy was running out of energy. Regeneration had a cost, and Gutsy couldn't pay forever.

Gutsy struggled on the ground, awful, wet noises of pain and anguish coming from the mangled body of the mascot. The blades of the machine didn't reveal foam and rubber, but wet meat inside the outer shell of the costume, red and black and viscous, but Gutsy didn't reach for him anymore. It was trying to put itself back together.

It reached for the pieces of flesh flung apart.

"Hurry!" yelled Shannon. "Grab him! While he's trying to recover."

Shannon jumped off the machine and grabbed Gutsy by pieces of his fur, and Tom clutched his feet, and they dragged the creature to the rear of the zamboni, on the platform at the back of the vehicle. Gutsy was heavy, but together they half dragged him up there, and dumped him. Gutsy struggled in their grasp, but couldn't stop them.

"He's hurt," said Tom. "Let's go!"

"Don't let him fall off," said Shannon.

Tom wrapped his hand around Gutsy's wrist, still in one piece. Just touching him felt wrong, but he couldn't let him go, not now. They were almost done with this.

Shannon jumped behind the wheel and floored the accelerator. The zamboni sped to its top speed. It wasn't fast, but they weren't going far. Something inside the vehicle clunked and then rattled. He was sure driving over a mascot wasn't good for the machine, but they only needed it to make it another hundred feet.

Tom kept an eye on Gutsy. He still held on, even as Gutsy slowly pieced himself back together. His flesh slid back and forth across itself, slowly pushing itself into one piece again. They didn't have much time.

"How much longer?" asked Tom.

"Just thirty more seconds," said Shannon.

"I don't know if we have that long," said Tom. He wasn't sure if he should keep touching the creature. Every moment, Gutsy regained strength, reaching into that void, into the well deep inside, and using it to heal himself. They had to hurry.

The zamboni slid to a halt.

"We're here," said Shannon. She jumped off and they grabbed Gutsy again. He struggled more.

"Fuck!" yelled Tom. They dragged him off the zamboni, even as he tried to fight them. His ripped and cut body was piecing itself back together.

"We're almost there," said Shannon, as they moved past the machine, to the impromptu target they had placed on the floor. They both breathed hard, but then Gutsy was on the target.

"Hurry," said Tom. "Turn the machine on." He held Gutsy down, with all his force. Only a few more seconds.

Shannon ran to the machinery and looked at Tom.

"Ready?"

"Hit it," said Tom. As soon as the machine was about to fire, he'd jump out of the way.

Shannon pushed the button, and the engine thrummed to life. It vibrated, shook, and powered up. As soon as the aperture glowed, Tom would move. Gutsy would be sent back.

It hummed louder and louder, and the blood drained out of the ampules, and then the aperture glowed red, a faint light at first, and then brighter. Tom let go of Gutsy, and went to move out of the way, far from the target zone, when something wrapped around him.

Gutsy's hand, his massive mitt, gripped hard around Tom's ankle.

Gutsy hadn't reformed, his legs still ruined, and his torso shredded, but his head had reformed, and his arm, and he stared at Tom, his hand holding him close.

You will not escape me. If I will be banished, you will come with me.

Tom kicked at Gutsy, but it did nothing. The aperture glowed brighter and brighter.

Shannon moved closer, but Tom put out a hand. "No, stay away," said Tom. "It's too dangerous." Gutsy held tight, even as Tom struggled, and the machine thrummed louder and louder.

You will see my home. You will see Hell.

Tom scanned the area frantically, looking for anything he could use. There was nothing. Nothing within reach, and Gutsy held him with an iron grip.

The aperture grew brighter still, and the machine was on the verge of shaking itself apart. It would activate any second now.

You will see. You will see.

"Tom!" yelled Shannon, and he looked, and she tossed him something, and he recognized it in midair. It was an ice skate.

The blade.

Tom snatched it out of the air, and brought the blade down hard on Gutsy's wrist. It cut through his flesh, and Tom forced it through, and Gutsy's hand was cut off, and Tom dove, the engine vibrating harder and harder, and then activating, the aperture glowing bright red, the light filling the space.

I will find my way back. I have seen this world. I will return.

Tom's eyes were closed, and the machinery thrummed, and he could see red, even through his closed eyes, and Gutsy's voice yelled out above the machine, above the light, above everything.

I will find my way back.

And then the light was gone, and the machine turned off, and they were alone.

26

Tom and Shannon sat in the small room. They'd been separated and held when the police arrived. They had agreed to not tell the police anything. There was no proof of them committing any crimes. Only security footage of them fighting a big mascot. What could the cops do?

But they'd been kept separate for hours now. When was it? Had to be after dawn, by this point.

Tom raised his eyebrow when he saw Shannon in the interrogation room, and was confused even further when the cop left them alone in there.

They exchanged a glance, but still said nothing. Someone was listening in, assuredly. They would have found the footage from the arena cameras. Of someone in a mascot costume on a rampage, killing nearly a dozen people. Of the pair of them fighting the mascot. Running it over with a zamboni, and using the transporter to send it—somewhere.

They would have questions. But if Tom and Shannon kept their mouth shut, they would have no proof of anything, and eventually, they'd let them go.

A few minutes passed, long enough for Tom to wonder how long they'd be kept here, when a man in a black suit entered the room. He wore dark Ray-Bans, was slender, with short hair, cut neatly. Nothing much else stood out, probably on purpose.

He closed the door behind him, and then took off the sunglasses, tucking them into his jacket pocket. His eyes looked tired. The man glanced at the two of them, back and forth, appraising them, and then sat down opposite them. He took his phone out of his pocket, and laid it on the table. Tom glanced at it. It was recording their conversation.

"What a shitshow," he said, looking at them. "It's getting worse." He sighed and rubbed the bridge of his nose. "You two are lucky I live in DC. Otherwise, you'd be in jail right now." They said nothing.

"Where did you get the Dawkins Machine?" asked the man. "I don't think you built it. The camera show you arriving with the thing, and setting it up. You knew how to operate it, at least on a rudimentary level." He stared at them, waiting for an answer. Tom said nothing, and Shannon stayed silent next to him.

"Jesus, guys, you can talk," said the man. "I'm not the cops, and they're not listening anymore. Or at least, they better not be. You're not going to jail. After we talk, you're free to go. Provided you cooperate."

"Who are you?" asked Shannon, finally.

"Agent Stuart Bowman," he said.

"FBI?" asked Shannon.

"No," said Bowman. "I'm not at liberty to say who I work for."

"What did you call the transporter? A Dawkins Machine?" asked Tom.

"It's the work of John Dawkins," said Bowman. "We thought we had nipped it in the bud, got rid of all of them. But you have one."

Tom remembered then, the recordings of Claypool. He had mentioned Dawkins.

"It was in the workshop of an artist, named Norman Claypool. He built it. He had gotten some of Dawkins' notebooks. Pieced it together from that," said Tom.

"Tom, don't tell him—"

"He knows something about this, Shannon," said Tom. "Look at him. He's not a cop."

"Claypool?" asked Bowman. "Never heard of him."

"He designed Gutsy," said Shannon. "He's dead. You'll find what's left of his body in his workshop."

Bowman glanced at her and thought for a second. "I see. He summoned Gutsy?"

"Well, he summoned something," said Tom. "It wasn't Gutsy until it got here."

Bowman nodded. "Adaptive interplanar creature. What a nightmare."

"You've seen these things before?" asked Shannon.

"Well, things like it," said Bowman. "Hard to say if they were the same or not. Lab guys might be able to test it, and verify, but it seems like Gutsy was too volatile to capture. You did the right thing, sending it back."

"What's going to happen?" asked Tom.

"What do you mean?" asked Bowman.

"To us," said Tom. "All those people, dead. You can't tell everyone the truth."

"You weren't here tonight," said Bowman. "Neither of you."

"But the cameras—"

"Footage is gone," said Bowman, staring at them. "We have it all. No one saw you. Everyone died."

"You can't just hide those deaths—"

"Serial killer," said Bowman. "Dressed as Gutsy. Escaped in the night."

"But, won't that scare people?" asked Tom.

"Sure," said Bowman. "But people will believe it. And there won't be any more killings. And people will forget. Move onto the next thing."

"What do we do?" asked Tom.

"Keep your mouth shut," said Bowman. "I can get you a stipend, for your work."

"Wait a minute, you're paying us?" asked Shannon.

"What, you don't want it?" asked Bowman.

"Well, I didn't say that," said Shannon.

"Okay then," said Bowman. "I don't think I have any more questions for you. Go home, get some rest." Bowman grabbed his phone, and shoved it into a pocket. He put his sunglasses back on.

"Wait," said Tom.

"What?" asked Bowman.

"You said it's getting worse, when you walked in," said Tom. "What do you mean? What's getting worse?"

Bowman stopped for a second. He paused. Finally, he

spoke. "The stuff I deal with. There seems to be more of it, lately. I don't know. I can't—"

"You're not at liberty to say," said Shannon.

"You got it," said Bowman.

"What do we do, if we need to talk to you?" asked Tom.

Bowman looked back at them, standing at the door.

"You don't."

*

Bowman was right. People did forget.

Gutsy was retired, after the killings. They could have had another costume made, but the PR team knew they'd get roasted for using the serial killer mascot, despite how much publicity it'd get them. Instead, they got a new mascot, one with a safer appearance. It was a fish from the Baltimore harbor. The new mascot was called Blueford, the bluegill. It also wasn't as nearly as popular as Gutsy, but honestly, it was for the best.

Tom and Shannon both kept working for the Brawlers, alternating playing Blueford, just like they used to with Gutsy. They just didn't have to worry about Blueford coming to life after they went home for the night. They had a memorial for all the victims of Gutsy, including Cloudy and Skates, and they hung a banner in the arena for them.

But life moved on, and people forgot.

Tom sat in the break room, the head of Blueford on the table in front of him, much like Gutsy used to sit. He stared into the eyes of Blueford. Nothing there.

"You alright?" asked Shannon. She was packing up, ready to go home.

"Yeah," he said. They didn't talk much about Gutsy. And Tom didn't have the nightmares, not anymore. He knew Shannon had stopped taking the sleeping pills and the mood stabilizers. She seemed in a better place. He didn't want to bring it up, not after what they'd been through.

"You sure?" asked Shannon. She looked at him. "The way you're staring at that head—you're not having nightmares again, are you?"

"Oh no," said Tom. "No visions. No weird personality shifts. Nothing strange at all."

"Good," said Shannon.

"But it's hard not to expect it, after everything," said Tom. "I just keep remembering what Gutsy said. That he'd be back. And despite everything—I still think about it."

"You said it yourself. No visions. No nightmares. Most importantly, no more killings. And remember, Gutsy didn't get here on his own. Claypool had to bring him here. No one else has those machines. Doesn't really matter if Gutsy wants to come back or not. He can't travel on his own. And frankly, this fish doesn't look the part."

Tom looked back at the dopey eyes of Blueford. Shannon was right.

"You need help with the suit?" asked Shannon.

"You can go," said Tom. "I'll lock up."

Shannon went home, and Tom changed back into his street clothes. He piled Blueford back in the utility closet. Right where Gutsy used to lie. Tom stared at the costume. It didn't move. It didn't shift. No dark, wet voice rose from it. It was just a costume.

Tom turned off the lights and shut the door.

He left. The parking lot was mostly empty this late, and

he was alone, walking back to his car.

He heard a shuffling noise behind him, and he turned.

There was nothing.

Tom sighed and turned back.

He heard the noise again.

He didn't turn.

It was nothing.

It was nothing.

Sign up for TWO free, ex-clusive novels!

Sign up for Robbie's newsletter! Monthly sneak peeks at upcoming projects, cover teases, and instant access to TWO FREE, EXCLUSIVE novels!

www.robbiedorman.com/newsletter

About the Author

Robbie Dorman believes in horror. Killer Hockey Mascot is his eleventh novel. When not writing, he's podcasting, playing video games, or petting cats. He lives in Texas with his wife, Kim.

You can follow Robbie on Twitter @robbiedorman

Acknowledgements

Thank you to my wife Kim, for her patience and support. Thank you to my team of beta readers; Andrew, Matt, Megan, and Yousef, for your guidance and help. Thank you, for reading.

www.ingramcontent.com/pod-product-compliance
Lightning Source LLC
Chambersburg PA
CBHW030931210726
48290CB00007B/2155